MAMAW

By Dr. Minette Bryant

For Sally Marie Finkle

Table Of Contents

Chapter One

At first, the hole in the floor wasn't even noticeable. Of course, there was a rug in that spot, just as there was a rug in every spot that Mamaw considered a place of heavy foot traffic. Those grandkids could really tromp through the place and if one was going to keep the carpets clean, one had to have rugs down to protect it. The rugs were a mismatch of different colors and patterns and fabrics, all collected over the course of several decades, such that if the idea were to keep the carpet pretty, well…perhaps they worked, but as no one could see the carpet for all the mismatched rugs, the point was fairly moot. The floor of Mamaw's trailer looked like an enormous patchwork quilt that had forgotten, at some point along the way, what it had intended to become when it set out stitching itself together. Still, Mamaw was comforted to know that her carpet, though more than 30 years old, was clean and pretty under there. Or at least she thought so.

Those grandkids though. What a caution! Mamaw was always having to say, "Slow down! You're shaking the fish!" Her poor little aquarium in the corner would just slosh and rock when the kids ran through. Even after she passed the aquarium on to her grandson Troy for his college dorm room, that was still the thing to let the kids know they were being too rambunctious. "Slow down! You're shaking the fish!"

Of course, Mamaw had given that little aquarium to Troy …what was it now? Twenty some-odd years ago, and the grandkids weren't kids anymore. Some of them had kids of their own. They didn't shake the fish, the great grandbabies. They didn't shake anything. They never came.

Well, not never. They came for a visit about once a year, each little family coming separately to sit politely in her living room, fidgeting a little while they struggled for topics of conversation. The great grandkids would seek any excuse to get away, to go outside and sit with those things on their ears listening to the most awful stuff they called music. Their parents would dutifully sit there, stating repeatedly in different ways how the old place hadn't changed at all, and surreptitiously glancing at their watches and then at each other as if each hoping the other would have the perfectly crafted excuse to leave as quickly as possible. Perhaps someone left the stove on at home, or the dog needed to be tended. Any minor medical emergency would do nicely.

Sometimes the children outside would provide the escape route: a bee sting, a scraped knee, a nosebleed. Once, Troy's oldest girl, Meg, had taken Mamaw's telephone back into the bedroom, snaking the long, twisted avocado-green cord almost the whole length of the trailer, to call up three or four of her middle school girlfriends for a chat rather than visiting with Mamaw. About an hour into the visit, she came bursting from the room in hysterical convulsions of sobbing, having learned that her boyfriend of the last two weeks was breaking up with her for another girl, Jenny, because "Jenny dyed her hair like Cindy Looper!" Mamaw didn't learn any more about Jenny or Cindy Looper, as that maniacal teenage upset was the escape route the family had been seeking. All she learned as they walked their sobbing child to the car, was that they were the worst parents in the world, having denied their daughter the right to dye her own hair, and that Jenny was never going to be allowed to borrow Meg's glitter mousse again.

Mamaw often shook her head a little, as though to clear the cobwebs, when she thought of the words "great grandchildren." Not only because the children weren't all that great, but also because that meant that she, herself, was a great-grandmother. Great grandmothers, she knew, were very, very old. Of course, she woke up with aches and pains every morning for years now, and she never could stay awake long enough to watch the ten o'clock news…and didn't understand any of it when she could. Forensically, she understood that the world had changed drastically, that 1987 was very different from 1917, when she herself had been a youngster…only in 1917, children still cherished their grandparents, and everything made a lot more sense. When Mamaw slept, she sometimes revisited her childhood, saw herself as nine or ten years old, running through her own grandparents' pasture, chasing butterflies, or working in the kitchen alongside her mother, making biscuits for the big lunch that had to be prepared for the men coming in from the field.

She dreamed of her grandmother's big screen porch where she would sit for hours with her mother and her aunts, shelling peas or snapping beans or shucking corn. It was always such a delight when she would find, buried in the green skin of a large ear of corn, another tiny baby ear of corn, no bigger than her finger…and she would eat it right there on the porch, cob and all. In all her years of shucking corn, she'd only found maybe four of those perfect little treats, and those moments were more special to her than if she'd found a pirate's chest.

Many years later, when she and Papaw were dating, he took her for her first meal in a Chinese restaurant and there, in her mixed vegetables were at least a dozen of those tiny baby corns, and all Mamaw could imagine was a humongous screened in porch full of Chinese children, all furiously shucking corn, the piles of green shucks and golden silks piling up to the ceiling fans, and every once in a while, one of them would jump up and shout triumphantly, "I got one! I got one!" Knowing what a treasure every one of those tiny corns must be, Mamaw savored each one of them that night, and even decades later, when she could buy big jars of them in the supermarket and she fully understood how they were grown that way, she still pictured the enormous porch full of Chinese children every time she ate one.

Sometimes she dreamed of herself as older, in her late teens and early twenties, when the young men paid attention to her and she laughed with pleasure and placed her hand on their arm, knowing full well that it meant much more to them than it did to her. She walked in high heels and chose skirts that hugged her figure. She was never what they called a Flapper, but she did love the long strings of beads, and she did love to dance. It was at a local dance that she met Papaw. He was so handsome, with hair like the corn silks she had loved as a child.

She knew right away that he would be the man she married. He knew it too. That night. She often dreamed of that night, how she saw him gazing at her from across the room, and how she glided toward him like the pull of a magnet, how they molded their bodies together for a slow dance without even speaking, and without ever breaking eye contact.

At least that's the way she dreamed it. If the reality, so long ago, wasn't quite that poetic, what did it matter now? Papaw had been gone since 1955, and she could damn well dream him any way she wanted to at this point.

Mamaw never dreamed of herself as eighty years old, stooped over with enormous bat wings of skin hanging under each arm. She didn't dream the cracking voice that she heard issuing from her own mouth, nor the absence of several teeth, nor the thin silver hair that she had long ago ceased arranging in a 1940's style. In her dreams she was never wearing any one of her series of shapeless button up house dresses that hung nebulously over her thin frame in much the same way that the saggy skin hung underneath the house dress.

She had read once that the skin is the largest organ of the human body. If her skin was an organ, then it had once been one of those tiny Hammond organs, perfect and compact and able to produce the loveliest variety of musical tones…but now it was more along the lines of an ancient pump organ, wheezing out gusts of sound nobody wanted to listen to anymore, and rotting in the corner of some ruined church, just waiting for the weather and the weeds to do it in.

Her single wide trailer had two small bedrooms and one bath; There was a mirror hanging over the vanity table in the guest room, but the one in Mamaw's bathroom had long ago been replaced with a cheap print of Van Gogh's sunflowers. She found it much cheerier to brush her few remaining teeth looking at that image every morning rather than her own. She never went into the guest room anymore anyway. No point. She never had guests who stayed. The sheets were clean at least…she hadn't needed to change them in seven years since the night Troy asked her to babysit Meg so that he and his wife could go out of town. So, she figured, if there were to suddenly be overnight company, the guest room was always ready.

Her mobile home was more than thirty years old now. She had bought it in the year after Papaw had died. There had been many reasons, but ultimately it just made sense to sell the big house. The kids were both out on their own now, and it was just too much trying to manage the big house, paying the mortgage and paying the taxes. Her daughter helped her sell the house, and with the equity plus Papaw's life insurance, she was able to buy outright a 1955 Terra-Cruiser mobile home with all the modern amenities, and an acre of land to set it on. Terra-Cruiser's ad in *Look* magazine said, "You'll be living in 1995 when you live in a 1955 Terra-Cruiser!" Well, it was eight years yet until 1995, and Mamaw was still in her Terra-Cruiser.

…her Terra-Cruiser, which was beginning to have the smallest, almost unnoticeable hole in the floor.

She first noticed it on a Thursday morning. It was right in front of the middle cushion of the living room sofa, right where Mamaw put her feet when she sat with her morning coffee to watch *Good Morning America*. This was her morning ritual partly because she couldn't manage to stay awake for the news at night, and partly—perhaps even mostly—because she had a long-standing crush on Charles Gibson. It was like a gift from the Universe that his move from nighttime news anchor to morning news anchor occurred concomitantly with her own organically shifting schedule.

People think that celebrity crushes go away when you're an octogenarian, but that's not true. Mamaw could have the most delicious fantasies about being interviewed by Charles Gibson, and she would laugh with feminine charm and place her hand on his arm and tell him…well, that part didn't matter. She didn't wonder what he might be interviewing her about. Surely something in her life was worth his time and attention. Hadn't there been that one time when the young man came to her door asking directions to the courthouse, and then proceeded to steal her lawnmower? She had given him directions—thinking what a nice young man he was—and then bid him good day and closed the door. A few seconds later she heard a clatter and opened the door again to see the nice young man bodily muscling her push mower into the back seat of his Buick. When she opened the door, he stopped what he was doing and they stared at each other for what felt like an eternity (though it was probably less than seven seconds) and then with one final shove, he managed to get the mower in, flung himself into the front seat and sped away. She hadn't said a word to him; but upon later reflection, she felt really brave for just standing there looking at him, looking him right in the eye. "He might have had a gun, Charlie!" she would say with wide eyes. "Why, my grandson Troy had just been using that mower two days before! What if the robber had come on THAT day? He might have tried to hurt Troy!"

In her daydream, she could hear the audience gasping at the possible horror and applauding in awe of her steadfast courage in the face of such an obvious threat to herself and her progeny. She might even muster up a tear as she thought of Troy, so vulnerable, depending on her bravery to save him from this menace…and then Charles Gibson, seeing the tear shining in her beautiful brown eyes, would be the one to place a compassionate hand on *her* arm…and most likely ask her to lunch after the show for further discussion about her impressive character and fortitude.

In her daydream interview, Mamaw generally left out that the lawnmower story happened in 1975, and of course, in this daydream (as in her night dreams), she was still a lovely little Hammond organ, wearing long beads and a skirt that hugged her figure.

"Charlie," she would say coquettishly, "That's so sweet of you to say. I never think of myself as an intellectual, but I certainly won't disagree with you. I went to college for a year before I got married— my husband is long gone you know—but these days I like to read, and I know that helps to keep the mind sha…wait…what is this? Seems like a worn place in the carpet under the rug…"

Reality had intruded upon her fantasy, and she had to leave imaginary Charlie sitting, quietly adoring her in front of a live studio audience, while she investigated the odd little soft spot she had just found with the big toe of her left foot.

The spot right in front of the sofa was definitely a high traffic area, as Mamaw got up and down from this spot several times a day. First thing in the morning for Charlie, then again at noon for the first of her soaps, *Ryan's Hope*, then up and down for the next four hours as she kept up with the stories through the whole ABC line-up: *Loving*, *All My Children*, *One Life to Live*, and *General Hospital*. These were her family now; she knew them much better than she knew her children or her grandchildren or her great-grandchildren.

She could count on them to always be there, to always be predictable, to always be interesting, and to always include her as they played out the drama of their lives. Mamaw was daily sucked into a world where most everyone has an evil twin and at least one long lost child (who no doubt *also* has an evil twin), where they all live in mansions and are CEOs of unwaveringly successful companies, and yet no one seemed to have a job or responsibility outside of meddling in everyone else's business, and having super-secret confidential discussions in some public place where they could be overheard by exactly the wrong person such that they would be fully exposed within the next five episodes, and usually when someone was already in her wedding dress ready to walk down the aisle to whatever man she's just learned the dastardly truth about.

But on this day, Mamaw was far more interested in the soft spot under the rug than in whatever Erica Kane might be wearing for her umpteenth murder trial. With untold difficulty, she slid off the couch and crouched on the floor, lifting the corner of the dollar-store rug that protected the carpet in that spot. Expecting to see that the basically brand new 30-year-old carpet was simply flattened from her feet over the years, she was instead surprised to find an actual little hole all the way through the floor, such that she could peer down through it to the sparse grass below.

The fact she had detected it with her big toe might well have been because the diameter of the hole was about the size of her big toe; about the size of a quarter. Of course, Mamaw knew, logistically, that her trailer was 32 years old, but it hadn't really ever occurred to her that—as she went about her daily business, waking, sleeping, bathing, baking, being interviewed by Charles Gibson or on trial with Erica Kane—her house-on-wheels was quietly decaying. Crouched there on the floor, peeping down at the grasshopper who was grooming himself in what he believed was privacy, it occurred to

Mamaw that the Terra-Cruiser *Look* magazine ad had been a lie. This house wasn't going to make it to 1995.

Chapter Two

The sign hanging on the wall beside the motel check-in desk said, "NO SMOKING IN PUBIC AREAS." Well, hell...he wasn't going to do that anyway. Not that he even smoked at all, or had ever been able to see the allure of it, but the unfortunate misspelling on the sign led him, unwittingly, to a number of odd imaginings of how one might smoke with one's pubic areas and, finally incensed by the pornographic offerings of his own subconscious, he wondered if perhaps the spelling of the sign had been intentional. This was, after all, the sort of motel that catered to the kind of clientele who might find titillating the very images he had just pushed away.

The night manager finally returned to the desk and, without ever looking at him, she simply said, "Yeah?"

Ralph shook off the last vestiges of the pubic-area-smoking-imagery from his head and braced his hands on the worn counter. "You got a guest named Brashear."

"Who's askin?" the clerk drawled, loudly chomping her gum and still not looking up from her papers on the desk.

"I'm not asking," Ralph said impatiently, "I'm telling you straight up, you got a guest named Brashear." While he explained, he extracted his badge from his pocket and flashed it at her. Over the years, he'd become remarkably adept at tilting his badge just so that the light in any room would catch and flash against the metal shield. After all, what was the point of *having* a badge if you couldn't display it impressively? Impressively...but nonchalantly. That was Ralph's personal mantra. Get their attention, but act like you couldn't care less about their attention.

Even in the buzzing fluorescence of this dingy motel office, the trick worked. Blinded for a millisecond, the previously disinterested clerk looked up and met Ralph's gaze at last. "Sorry, officer…" (she looked more closely at the ID card in its little plastic holder) "Officer James."

"Detective," he corrected her.

"Detective James," she repeated, and smiled. Or grimaced. Hard to tell in this lighting. Either way, she was not what he would call attractive in any sense of the word. She was probably in her mid-thirties, but the tell-tale signs of a long-term relationship with nicotine and malt liquor made her look more like a hardened fifty, and her insistence on maintaining hair the color of ripe strawberries had left it the texture of an old Halloween witch wig that Ralph had once worn in a high school production of Shakespeare's Macbeth. Looking at this clerk, he could almost feel the sweat beading on his scalp under that itchy wig. To complete the classic-witch look, her long bony fingers, knuckles swollen from years of cracking them needlessly, were tipped with K-Mart press-on nails in lime green. She hadn't bothered to file them, and Ralph could still see the little tabs on the sides of each nail where she had punched them out of the packaging. She had probably applied them about two weeks ago, as he could see her natural nails grown about an eighth of an inch between her cuticle and the lime green press-ons. Upon closer inspection, he observed that the plastic nail was missing from her right ring finger, and she had bitten her real nail so deeply to the quick that it had bled. Perhaps biting her singular exposed nail was how she kept anxiety at bay while waiting for a chance to get away from the no-smoking sign for a few minutes every hour or so.

In TV cop dramas, seedy motel managers were always deeply invested in protecting the identity of their customers, insisting they'd offer no information without a warrant, and not complying with warrants even if there was one. But in real life, Ralph always found motel clerks to be much more interested in gossip than confidentiality. This was a truly dull job, and it didn't pay anyone enough to keep their mouths shut, especially to cops. When a cop showed up at a place like this, it almost certainly meant a juicy story to take home to the kiddies, and there was no license or certification or bar that might be taken away from a motel clerk who told tales.

The clerk stuck her hand through the little window for Ralph to shake, which he did, but not too hard lest he cause undue pain to the critically bitten ring fingernail. "Carmilla," she said, and Ralph assumed it was her name.

"Carmilla," Ralph repeated, withdrawing his hand from the obligatory embrace. "You got a guest here named Brashear."

Carmilla leaned forward over the counter conspiratorially. "Yeah," she whispered, smacking her gum, her eyes growing large in anticipation of the gory details of whatever criminal activity Brashear might have been involved in. "He came in here yesterday…looks like trouble. Handsome, you know? The kind of handsome that uses his powers for evil. I don't go for that type myself. I like good guys, you know?" With that, she turned her head slightly and looked at Ralph from the corner of her eye so that, yes, he definitely knew.

"Can I have a key?" Ralph asked.

This was another thing…on TV, cops were always breaking down doors of motel rooms and cheap apartments, but Ralph had never had any proprietor refuse to just give him a key. Sure saved a lot of timber…and a lot of muscle pain in the morning. What business owner wants his doors kicked in, dealing with the insurance hassle, trying to get reimbursed by the department?

Nobody. There's always an extra key.

Carmilla pushed away from the counter. "What'd he do? Drugs?" she asked. "Murder?" The tone of her voice grew more anticipatory as her imagination kicked in.

"Theft," Ralph said simply.

"Ooo..." Carmilla handed him the shiny brass key she had pulled from the rack on the wall. "Like a bank robbery? Hide out in a place like this and no one would suspect you got cash, that's for sure!"

"No," Ralph said, taking the key, "Last night he walked out of the Grandy's restaurant with six whole roasted chickens smuggled in his pants. Camera caught him sneaking out of the kitchen. Video tape clearly shows the license plate of his car—the same car sitting out there in your parking lot, so here I am to pick him up."

"Six chickens...?" Carmilla's facial expression could have represented either her incredulity at learning of such a crime, or her amazement that a grown man with a badge had been sent to dispatch such an odd criminal.

On his way to room 204, Ralph thought about that. About being a grown man with a badge chasing down another grown man for smuggling six whole chickens in his pants. What kind of life was this anyway?

Well, it was the kind of life where he got to be a full detective in his thirties. When he started out on the force in Shreveport, he quickly realized that he would be a beat cop until he was fifty. It was a huge force, choked with good old boys looking out for each other and general nepotism. A guy without connections—a guy like Officer Ralph James—was highly unlikely to see promotion unless he found a way to really stand out in the field. Day after day for years, Ralph was standing in the middle of domestic disputes, or handcuffing guys in their underwear for selling weed from their living rooms, or pretending to take notes while some lady babbled on for an hour about the things she was just positive her neighbors were doing. Ninety percent of this Significant Police Work took place at the Fairmont Apartment Towers on Cotton Street. Ralph actually considered renting a room there himself once, just to make the midnight calls a quicker affair, but ultimately decided he'd be too much of a target, and the nosy old ladies would never leave him alone.

When Ralph was a kid, eleven or twelve years old, his younger sister Miriam had gotten into show bunnies. Like show dogs, only…rabbits. For a couple of years, about twice a month, his parents would load them up on a Saturday, fill the back of the station wagon with stackable rabbit cages, and drive anywhere from an hour to four hours so Miriam could show her bunnies. The events were always held in some giant barn filled with people who took this show bunny thing *very* seriously. Ralph understood Miriam's interest…she was a little girl and the only thing little girls love more than unicorns is bunny rabbits…but most of these people were adults, fully grown humans who, supposedly, had jobs and lives and responsibilities, and they *lived* for these bunny shows. He would see the same people at every show, watching the judges intently, grooming their rabbits just so. Ralph didn't understand it. It certainly looked like the rabbits didn't understand it.

Over those couple of years, little Ralph became quite knowledgeable about the different breeds being shown. Who knew there were so many kinds of rabbits? Lionhead rabbits, Flemish Giants, Continental Giants, English Lop, Holland Lop, French Lop, Mini Rex…Ralph's personal favorite was the Dwarf Hotot, always solid white with what looked like Cleopatra black eyeliner. As far as he could see, there wasn't any regular sized Hotot, so he wasn't sure why it was called the Dwarf Hotot. Still, it was his favorite.

When Miriam started down this rabbit hole, no pun intended, she had a pair of Jersey Woolies. Jersey Woolies are very small rabbits with long soft hair and a big funny puff of it on top of their heads. Jersey Woolies are absolutely the next best thing to unicorns. Miriam would cuddle them and brush their long hair and decorate them with barrettes and bows…of course the look in the rabbits' eyes said, "Please god deliver us from our tormentor" but Miriam was thrilled with her bunny babies.

The thing is, as much as Miriam loved her Jersey Woolies, so did *everyone else* love their Jersey Woolies, and so on show day, when the Jersey Woolies were called for their judging, Miriam proudly carried her two babies to be entered alongside at least forty other Jersey Woolies, most of them being shown by hardened professionals who would, Ralph had been disturbed to learn, literally eat any rabbit that wasn't showing well.

There were generally four awards to be given: trophies for Best of Group and Best Opposite (meaning that if Best of Group was given to a male, then Best Opposite would be given to the highest rated female and vice versa) and then ribbons for second and third place. With forty Jersey Woolies in the group, Miriam was *never ever* going to take home an award of any kind.

Being the youngest of the bunny show regulars, Miriam gained a group of adult friends who occasionally offered her advice on the care and grooming and showing of her bunnies. One day, Miriam came running to her father to say that one of the breeders was offering to just give her a pair of Polish rabbits, as the breeder was not going to be focusing on Polish anymore. Miriam was thrilled! More bunnies!

On that very day, when Miriam was being gifted more bunnies, the Polish group had not yet been called, so Miriam's father hurried to enter her two new bunnies in their category. When the group was called, and Ralph dutifully followed her sister to the area for that group, he was shocked to see that there were only three other Polish rabbits in the contest besides Miriam's new bunnies.

Polish rabbits are not large, but they're also not small—not like Jersey Woolies or Dwarf Hotots. They have soft hair, but it is not long and fluffy. The distinctive feature of the Polish is that its ears are short and stumpy in comparison to the classic long eared rabbit. They were cute, but not "oh my gosh would you look at that" like Ralph had heard a million times gasped over Miriam's Jersey Woolies. But that day, for rabbits she hadn't even owned long enough to name yet, Miriam took home trophies for both Best of Group and Best Opposite.

After that, the Jersey Woolies stayed home. They still got brushed and cuddled, to their perpetual chagrin, but the Polish went to the shows, and Miriam's dad had to build a special shelf for her trophies. Because there were so few people interested in Polish, there were far fewer entries in any given show, and so Miriam was assured at least a ribbon in every competition, whereas with the incredibly popular Jersey Woolies, she was simply never going to win.

Ralph remembered this lesson when he was an unknown beat cop in Shreveport. He worked with guys who had been on the job for twenty years and were still working traffic or standing in the rain directing cars after a concert at the Hirsch. If he was going to make detective before retirement, he was going to have to go Polish.

He did that by transferring to the precinct in Cotton Gorge. Cotton Gorge Louisiana had a population of 963, compared to Shreveport's 190,000. The Shreveport police department was made up of about a thousand officers, in Cotton Gorge, that number was two.

Two.

And right away, newly promoted Detective Ralph James knew he was easily holding the trophy for Best of Group.

The cases he worked in Cotton Gorge were basically the same as he'd managed in Shreveport: petty theft, petty drugs, domestic disputes, drunk and disorderly; but in Cotton Gorge, he was doing it all in a suit rather than a uniform, and even if the people had no noticeable increase of respect for his new title, Ralph had an increase of respect for himself.

He quietly bolstered this self-respect as he turned the key in the lock of room 204, and opened the door to come face to face with a man in his underwear who was polishing off a greasy chicken carcass while watching a rerun of *Bewitched* on the small black and white television. Frozen with his plastic fork halfway to his mouth, the man stared at Ralph as Ralph noted with his peripheral vision the other chicken carcasses piled in the tiny motel trash can and the oversized grey sweatpants drip-drying over the tub in the back.

Finally the man spoke: "You wanna bite?"

Chapter Three

Almost cherishing the anxiety it brought her, Mamaw left the little hole uncovered. Even ten years ago, she might have called one of the kids to come see how it might be fixed…but not now. When a seventy-year-old woman in a twenty-year-old mobile home had a hole in her floor, it could be fixed and forgotten. When an *eighty*-year-old woman in a *thirty*-year-old mobile home had a hole in her floor, it became a long, hushed conversation amongst the family about whether it wasn't simply time for a nursing home.

She remembered visiting her own grandmother in a nursing home and thinking how horrible it must be to have to live there. The unending smell of physical decomposition and antiseptic, the constant moaning sounds coming from every corner of the building. Now she had to wonder how much those things would actually bother her, since her hearing and her sense of smell were so dulled by time. If she had her own room, she could keep the door closed and the TV turned up…but still, she'd have to eat the food they served and follow the rules and the timing of the facility. Mamaw really liked being on her own. She wasn't ready to lose her independence.

Charles Gibson never interviewed anyone in a nursing home. Their lives didn't lend themselves to any newsworthy activities. She needed more time.

It was Sunday, and none of her television family would be visiting today, so Mamaw filled the day with her other favorite family member: Barry Manilow. In the corner of the living room there sat an enormous console stereo that had been a gift from her son in 1972. It had a radio tuner, a reel-to-reel tape player, and a record player. When it was closed, it made a lovely piece of furniture for holding various knick-knacks, but when opened, it offered the most beautiful music that filled the space of her small trailer.

It hadn't been opened in about twelve years. Too much trouble.

But among the knick-knacks collected on the surface of the console was a small portable rectangular cassette player with a single tinny speaker, and beside the player was a stack of three cassette boxes: *Even Now*, *Barry Manilow II*, and *This One's for You*. Over the years, she had been gifted many other Barry Manilow albums and collections, but these were the three she listened to over and over, the ones she had memorized. These were the three that were her closest friends.

Barry Manilow always had a song that could underscore whatever mood she was in. "Copa Cabana" when she wanted to jiggle her flesh a little; "Daybreak" when she was feeling like reveling in the life she'd led. "Mandy" when she wanted to think of the people she'd lost over the years; "Even Now" when she wanted to think about Charles Gibson.

Today she wanted to suffer a little over the hole in the floor and how it was a metaphor for the ebbing away of her life, so she opened the case of *This One's for You* and popped side two in the little player. With just a bit of expert fast-forward/rewind action, she cued up "All the Time."

All the time I thought there's only me, crazy in a way that no one else could be; I would have given everything I own if someone would have said "you're not alone." All the time I thought that I was wrong, wanting to believe but needing to belong; if I'd've just believed in all I had, if someone would have said "you're not so bad."

All the time, all the wasted time, all the years waiting for a sign. To think I had it all, all the time.

19

Perhaps this was a little *too* much suffering today. Mamaw found herself sobbing in huge uncontrollable convulsions that she imagined could easily lead to a cardiac event. A cardiac event *plus* a hole in the floor would surely mean immediate institutionalization. She stumbled back to the little cassette player and pushed the STOP button with so much force that the whole machine jumped as Barry stopped singing in astonishment.

Trying to control her breathing as the sobbing began to subside, Mamaw stepped backward from the stereo console toward the sofa and then yelped in surprise as a horrible pain seared through the bottom of her bare foot and up her leg like a bolt of electricity. The shock of the sudden pain made her lose her balance, but she was close enough to the sofa that her fall backward simply landed her in her favorite spot on the center cushion. Wondering what on earth she had stepped on to cause that much pain, Mamaw twisted her body as best she could to raise the bottom of her left foot into her line of sight, only to find the tiniest drop of blood beading there on the ball of her foot, just below the second toe.

Choosing to examine the floor now rather than her foot, Mamaw saw something so strange that she had to take a moment to even understand what she was seeing. There was now no hole in the floor, but instead, the newly uncovered cream-colored carpet was unbroken as her gaze swept across it. She couldn't even see where the hole had been...until she did. The slightest bit of movement drew Mamaw's watery eyesight to the place where the hole had been, the hole that was now filled with a nose...a nose with whiskers, protruding up through the little hole in her floor.

Suddenly astonishment turned to anger. All the time...all the wasted time...and now there were vermin trying to get into her house before she was even out of it. The tears of self-pity that she'd been nursing just moments before were now the mist of self-righteous indignation, and Mamaw did the one thing she thought anyone would do in this situation…she went for her broom.

With more force than anyone might have thought possible from a woman her age, Mamaw raised the broom high above her head and, the bat wings under her arms flapping ferociously, she beat and beat and beat at The Nose in her floor. All it took was one swipe for The Nose to disappear, but it took at least six swipes to satisfy Mamaw before she dropped the broom and leaned over with her hands on her knees to catch her breath. If this was the moment she would experience a cardiac event, bring it on. She would much rather die having defended her property, her life, her independence, than to die inconspicuously in a convalescent home, a half-finished bowl of tapioca quietly building a film on her nightstand.

When the adrenaline drained from her muscles, she realized just how much the ferocity of her attack on the invading nose had exhausted her. Mamaw wasn't really one for taking naps, but suddenly she needed one very badly.

That feeling of a surge of electricity up her left leg from the tiny wound on the bottom of her foot began throbbing back to life now that the fury of the assault was over. All the way up into her hip and then up her spine, she could feel the tingling sensation, but her exhaustion in that moment overwhelmed any medical curiosity she might have otherwise indulged. Besides, in her eighties, medical curiosities were her constant companion. If she gave each of them her due, how would she ever have the time to follow even one soap opera, let alone five? Limping only slightly on the damaged foot, Mamaw made her way to the bedroom, unmade the freshly made bed, and tucked herself in under the covers.

At first it was the music. There were no accompanying images as one might expect in a dream, just the blaring Barry Manilow music, even louder than Mamaw really liked it. He was practically shouting at her, "I MADE IT THROUGH THE RAIN! I KEPT MY WORLD PROTECTED!! LOOKS LIKE WE MADE IT!!! I'VE BEEN UP, DOWN, TRYING TO GET THE FEELING AGAIN!! AND I'M READY TO TAKE THE CHANCE AGAIN!!

In her fitful slumber, Mamaw groaned outwardly as in her inner world she was trying to keep up with the changing tunes, trying to sing along, trying to find Barry in the darkness. "COME! COME! COME INTO MY ARMS!!" he shout-sang at her and she could feel her whole body buzzing with electricity as she fumbled through the dream to find him.

"TELL ME, WHEN WILL OUR EYES MEET? WHEN CAN I TOUCH YOU??"

"I'm…I'm coming, Barry," she said feebly, feeling so lost and so tired, "I have to tell you what I did. I have to tell you about The Nose in the floor…"

Ever elusive, Barry's disembodied voice continued battering her with his power-ballad lyrics. "SOMEWHERE DOWN THE ROAD, OUR ROADS ARE GONNA CROSS AGAIN!! WE'RE JUST SHIPS THAT PASS IN THE NIGHT…!! COME WITH MEEEE…. SOMEWHERE IN THE NIGHT WE WILL KNOW EVERYTHING LOVERS CAN KNOW…!"

Mamaw could no longer feel her feet on the ground in her dream and she realized she was floating, propelled by that buzzing electrical feeling that coursed through every last one of her old rattling veins. She struggled for a moment, but then gave herself over to the floating and the buzzing, intermingled with the dramatic piano lines and big-band key modulations that made Barry's overbaked love songs so popular.

Then, suddenly, Barry's volume rose even higher as he began singing "IT'S DAYBREAK! IF YOU WANNA BELIEVE, IT CAN

BE DAYBREAK! AIN'T NO TIME TO GRIEVE, SAID IT'S DAYBREAK! IF YOU'LL ONLY BELIEVE AND LET IT SHINE SHINE SHINE ALL AROUND THE WORLD!!"

This announcement of morning couldn't have been more impactful if there had been an actual rooster landing on her coverlet to crow lauds. Mamaw popped awake in the bright sunlight streaming through the bedroom window of her Terra-Cruiser. Shocked that she had actually slept through the night, with no memory of waking to roll over when one hip or the other got tired of the pressure, or getting up for the bathroom and then a drink of water, which inevitably meant getting up later for the bathroom again. She was always dubious of people on TV who fell asleep on a sofa or at their desk at work and awoke the next morning, surprised at their surroundings (and usually with perfectly fresh hair and makeup). She hadn't slept all the way through the night since…well since never. Maybe at some point in childhood before her functional memory began, but she doubted even then.

She pulled back the covers and rolled herself into a sitting position, preparing to slip her feet into the fuzzy slippers that waited beside the bed, but the softest sound in the doorway caught her attention, and she looked up quickly.

There, lounging easily against the doorframe of her bedroom, stood Barry Manilow. Shaggy blonde hair, noteworthy nose, lanky frame, tight khaki jeans…and grinning lazily at her. Mamaw opened and closed her mouth repeatedly like a codfish desperately seeking a solid sip of oxygen. She stared at him, unblinking, until her eyes throbbed, but he just stood there, grinning, unconcerned and natural.

And then he started to sing.

In remembering it later, she honestly couldn't recall if there had been any sort of accompaniment, or if it had just been his voice.

23

His voice was all that mattered to her. His voice, and the song he chose.

"You are the woman," he crooned, standing out of his leaning position, but never coming any further into the bedroom, "that I've always dreamed of. I knew it from the start. I saw your face and that's the last I've seen of my heart. It's not so much your pretty face I see; it's not the clothes you wear. It's how I feel each time you're close to me, that always keeps me there…"

Barry never broke eye contact as he sang through this whole song. It was the most monumental moment of Mamaw's life. Her childhood, her marriage, the birth of her children and grandchildren…all rubbish compared to this glorious experience for which she had no camera and no witnesses. It didn't even matter to her that he was not singing an actual Barry Manilow song. This song, "You Are the Woman" was by Firefall, and she had always liked it. It was the sort of song she would hear playing softly in the background at the grocery store. Barry's version was even better than Firefall, though, and Mamaw was enthralled, trying to catch every nuance, trying to match Barry's smile. For the rest of her life, this song—this Barry Manilow version of this song which no one in the world but her would ever hear—would be her cherished favorite.

As the song was coming to an end, she began to be worried what to do once the singing stopped. Surely after the last note faded, the ball would be in her court. She should fix him breakfast or take him out somewhere fancy. She should surely have *something* to say. She wondered briefly if he'd ever had a lawnmower stolen right from under his nose. She wondered if he'd ever shucked corn.

But she needn't have worried about what she would say at all, because as his last note faded, Barry Manilow simply faded with it, still smiling, until he wasn't there at all.

…and in her astonishment, she awoke for the second time.

There was no light streaming in through the window of her Terra-Cruiser, because it was decidedly nighttime. The glowing orange numbers on the clock radio beside the bed said 6:58, and as her eyes focused on that number, the final eight broke in half and flipped itself with a tiny click to become a nine. Six fifty-nine. She must have slept through the afternoon and now would probably not sleep at all tonight.

But that was OK, because she had awakened with an idea for a craft project. Mamaw had not had a really good craft project idea in a very long time, but this was a hum dinger, and it wouldn't wait. Seven o'clock on a Sunday night meant that the local craft store was closed already, but most of what she thought she needed for this project was probably available at the regular grocery store, and they would still be open for another two hours. Plenty of time.

Mamaw hummed that Firefall song to herself as she straightened her rumpled house dress and slipped on her simple shoes. She felt that buzzing she'd felt through her dream, the floating dream. She felt a little floaty. She felt…excited somehow. Maybe because of her craft idea. Maybe because of Barry Manilow. Maybe she didn't need a reason. She was going shopping, and then she was going to sit up all night, fiddling with a needle and string and glue and who knows what else, making a personal masterpiece.

She felt, all of a sudden, very sure that life was good.

Chapter Four

Back in the late sixties, a man named Billy Hogan, an ambitious developer from Natchitoches, had bought a hundred twenty acres of pastureland in Cotton Gorge with the stated plan of creating a lake. He had signed all the correct forms and put billboards all over town announcing, "Cotton Gorge Lake: The Coolest Hot Spot in Louisiana!" These signs had pictures of families in bathing suits, building sandcastles together, or a picture of a lone fisherman sitting in a boat with his cap pulled over his eyes while his bobber floated a few feet away. This idea and the subsequent excitement had driven up the value of all the land surrounding the acreage that was to become the lake, and a number of investors from that part of the state had been determined to get in on the ground floor, buying up property to build lake-front housing developments. Billy Hogan himself had picked what he considered the absolute prime location and began construction on his lake house before the first bulldozer arrived to begin clearing for the lake. The town took this as a show of good faith.

But Billy Hogan disappeared in the fall of 1968. Just disappeared. Some of the more colorful stories included that he had misused funds from investors and, unable to repay them, he had moved to Dallas where he had been spotted once, by Cotton Gorge resident Deb Trahan, shopping for shoes at a Woolworths. Deb said he looked pretty good for a man down on his luck. Another story insisted that Billy had chosen an even better spot for his lake up in Helena, Arkansas, and if you drove up there, you'd see the exact same billboards that were still rather dilapidating in Cotton Gorge, only these proclaimed Lake Helena as "The Coolest Hot Spot in Arkansas."

The most persistent story was that Billy Hogan had been murdered by Artie Gomez, the cuckolded husband of his local girlfriend Marci Gomez, and was buried under the concrete foundation of his own lake house. Artie had never even been questioned in connection to this theory, but he and Marci moved to New Orleans shortly after the rumors began. There's nothing like small town gossip to send people packing.

Regardless of what became of Billy Hogan, the Cotton Gorge Lake never happened. The community had tried to bring it about after all, but between a general lack of cooperation and a general lack of funds, the project was perpetually "delayed." That's the word they used…delayed. It was too upsetting to call it canceled. It had been the only thing Cotton Gorge had ever pretended to offer that might put it on the map.

The single element of the Cotton Gorge Lake to hold on to the dream over the years was the speed trap.

That stretch of highway past the pastureland that would become the lake and the housing developments had historically had no speed limit. It was a long straight stretch of road and you were more likely to get stuck behind someone going 16 miles per hour on a tractor than to be in any kind of high-speed chase. However, the town had decided, in their gleeful anticipation of the lake and all the excitement it would breed throughout the state, that the traffic along that stretch of road would become absolutely choked with big-city folk used to driving the 70 miles an hour they were accustomed to, honking and yelling at one another as though trying to make it down Fifth Avenue in New York City. This idea was both thrilling and horrifying to the locals, and so a town hall meeting was held where it was decided to implement a 30 mile per hour speed zone to protect both locals and tourists in that area. The Cotton Gorge mayor, Paulie Schlaffer, used the word "tourists" eighty-three times in that town hall meeting, and it never failed to send a shiver of anticipation down the spine of each council member.

The town allocated fifty dollars to be spent on four new road signs: two announcing the 30 mph stretch, and two announcing the end of the 30 mph stretch. Standing there, so tall and shiny and official, these signs inspired local farmers, who rarely drove more than 20 miles per hour in their ancient wheezing pickup trucks, to push the peddle a little harder to get it up to exactly thirty on that road. People simply driving through Cotton Gorge on their way to Shreveport from Alexandria were often stymied by this new speed trap, and local police made more than fifty dollars in the first year—more than enough to cover the cost of the signs—by writing tickets to out of towners for violating the speed of the "Lake Zone."

Ralph came to serve in the Cotton Gorge police department in 1984, and the "Lake Zone" still had a posted speed limit of 30 miles per hour. By that time, traffic tickets for that zone brought in more revenue than any other single industry in Cotton Gorge. Every day, Ralph—ever interested in showing that he was not above the law—slowed to 30 mph as he neared the turnoff for the police headquarters, which was housed in Billy Hogan's abandoned lake house.

The lake house, or Hogan House as it had come to be called, had never been quite finished before Billy's disappearance. The exterior was completed at the time Hogan disappeared, but the inside had been left an empty gut of hanging ductwork and concrete floors. The city had tried to sell it, but no matter the house's potential, the fact that Hogan House was sitting, basically, in the middle of nowhere, made it quite unattractive to potential buyers. The persistent story that its original owner was murdered and buried under the foundation (this story was told in colorful detail to anyone who came to town with the slightest appearance of interest in the house) didn't help.

In 1972, the city quietly decided to save face by laying claim to the house and giving it a practical purpose. Hogan House had been originally designed as a four-bedroom, two bath ranch with a large living area, dining room, and modern kitchen. It was decided to finish it in basically that same style, though one bedroom was designed as a simple holding cell for the occasional miscreant, and the other three were sizable offices. The living room area was made into a plush meeting room, and the dining room became an all-purpose hall that could be rented out for any form of entertainment or gathering. This was a real winning point in the decision to make the house into a city building, the idea that renting out the all-purpose room would bring in more money for the city.

It had been rented out exactly six times in fifteen years.

The large kitchen area of Hogan House was finished as a reception area, with just a tiny apartment-style kitchenette on one end. Microwave, coffee pot, sink. The essentials for a police station. Hogan House had a lovely front entrance with heavy wooden double-doors, but no one used that entrance. Everyone entered through the side door into the kitchen/reception area, where the receptionist would greet them, find out what they needed, call the appropriate person, usher them to the meeting room, whatever was needed.

The Cotton Gorge police station receptionist was Desiree Ligety. Desiree had been the Cotton Gorge police station receptionist since 1955, and she was never going to let anyone forget how much nicer it was to do business out of the Hogan House than out of the 500 square foot trailer they had used before 1972. Desiree Ligety was never going to let anyone enter the Hogan House meeting room without wiping their feet. She had even been known to make someone remove their shoes entirely if she didn't believe wiping would be sufficient to protect the carpet. "You can track your little farm all over town on your own time, but not in this house!" To Desiree, this was *her* house, and the people of Cotton Gorge didn't dare contradict her.

Ralph was one of two officers in the Cotton Gorge department. His unlikely partner was Charles Farmer…whom everyone called Chili. Chili Farmer was a good old hometown boy who had spent more than one night in the Hogan House holding cell in his misspent youth but, as the town loved to tell it, the influence of a good woman had turned him around. Chili's wife Lydia had put him on the straight and narrow, and borne him four children in the five years since they married.

The town generally liked Chili, and Chili liked Ralph, which was helpful. It hadn't been easy coming into a small town and trying to establish authority. In Cotton Gorge, it was widely considered that anyone who lived north of Coushatta was a Yankee and therefore not to be trusted. Ralph wanted to be both friendly and aloof with the locals; "aloof" he could manage on his own, but for "friendly," he needed the support of Chili Farmer.

Chili and Desiree made up almost the entirety of Ralph's social life. If the city would have allowed it, Ralph would have happily moved a twin bed into his office and simply taken up residence at Hogan House…but he knew that was improper. Instead, he went home each night to his tiny apartment, one of ten units in the only apartment complex in Cotton Gorge, ate dinner in front of the TV, then slept until it was time to go back to work. On Saturdays he called his mother, and on Sundays he read a book, or went for a jog. At the grocery store, people he knew called him "Sir," and the local garage always charged him half price for an oil change. It was a pretty good life.

In the three years since Ralph came to Cotton Gorge, there had been very little development, but one major change happened right at the front of the road where he turned off the Lake Zone to drive out to Hogan House. A very plain, simple blue metal building had been erected on the corner. The town watched eagerly to see what it would become, and when the steeple was added at the very last of construction, excitement waned. For a town of less than a thousand, Cotton Gorge already had eight churches.

But this one turned out to be different. An incredibly gregarious young man calling himself Doctor Don began passing out flyers all over town, flyers with a picture of muddy boots and the slogan "The Lord Loves Your Overalls," offering to be the only one of Cotton Gorge's nine churches that would allow you to come to worship in your work clothes, no tie required. This changed things a bit. For a full month, Doctor Don filled his metal folding chairs with blue-jeaned congregants, and his offering baskets with their coinage, while the other eight churches went wanting. This looked like bad news, until Pastor Roland at the Second Methodist Church did a little sleuthing on Doctor Don.

It turned out that Doctor Don was actually Donald Ward of Columbia Mississippi, where he had served time for mail fraud and tax evasion after his attempt at establishing his church in that area. There was also a juicy story the Columbia Register newspaper secretary was more than anxious to tell Pastor Roland that had to do with a young woman in Doctor Don's flock who had loudly proclaimed herself to be the new incarnation of the Virgin Mary, carrying again the divine child through immaculate conception. Once born, the child, according to the story, showed no sign of divinity, but did look remarkably like Donald Ward, and the new Virgin Mary was currently living on food stamps and seeking child support, which is ostensibly why Doctor Don left the state to start over in Cotton Gorge.

Impressed with this level of detective work, Ralph wondered if Pastor Roland had perhaps chosen the wrong career for his skill set. There was no need to take out a newspaper ad or use any official channels to broadcast his findings; all Pastor Roland had to do was tell his wife what he had learned about Doctor Don, and by the following morning, everyone in Cotton Gorge was openly discussing it, and the church office was cleared out and empty.

The building stood empty for a while, but as it was an almost brand-new construction, it was no surprise to anyone the day the steeple came down and a sign went up that said "COMING SOON! POSSUM HOLE BAR AND GRILL."

Ralph now drove by the Possum Hole Bar and Grill every day on his way to work, but he had never been inside. He wasn't a bar and grill kind of guy. Plus, he figured it would be a buzz kill for the customers if the local Police Detective was hanging out there.

So, it was kind of a surprise the morning he came into the station and found a message waiting for him that the proprietor of the Possum Hole needed to see him.

Ralph had been called early that morning to go see a local farmer about some teenagers who had been playing hide and seek in his cornfield. Woodson McGuffee hadn't done any of his own farming in probably twenty years, but he liked to sit in a rocking chair at the edge of his field watching the work be done by the younger, more agile men he had hired. Every day, he hauled himself laboriously down from his farmhouse to the worn spot where the chair sat, and there he stayed most of the day in fair weather.

Woodson McGuffee was a big man, a very big man with noteworthy mobility issues, and he did not take kindly to his crops being used for sport by kids who could run around him three times and in between his legs before he could even get out of his chair to scold them. That morning, Ralph had taken detailed notes of Woodson's complaint, writing down the names of the teens the farmer was positive he could identify, and then he left Mr. McGuffee huffing loudly and lowering himself back into his chair.

Ralph had gone straight from home to McGuffee's farm that morning, so by the time he got into the office, it was nearly ten o'clock. He opened the door into the kitchen/reception area of Hogan House and loudly stomped his feet against the mat so that Desiree would know he was acceptable to walk through to his office. But Desiree wasn't at her desk.

"Where's Desiree?" he called into the meeting room, assuming Chili was somewhere within earshot, as his car was parked outside. Almost simultaneous to asking the question, Ralph cringed for a moment, knowing what the answer would be.

"Ligety split!" called Chili Farmer from his office.

This joke, this very bad joke, was Chili's favorite response to anyone and everyone who might inquire as to Desiree Ligety's whereabouts. In a town with a population of 963, it was doubtful that a single one of them had been spared this terrible pun. Even so, at least once a week, Ralph heard someone laugh politely at Chili's humor, as though the joke were in any way fresh.

Chili wandered into the reception area and leaned against the doorframe. "She said she had a dental appointment; said she told you last week."

Ralph grunted as he thumbed through the stack of mail on Desiree's desk. It mattered not whether she had told him. No one was calculating Desiree's hours. She was reliable to a fault, never left anything undone, and was usually both the first and the last person in the office every day. If anyone needed anything, a piece of evidence or a piece of information, Desiree Ligety could lay her hands right on it. She was an open encyclopedia of every person who lived or had lived in Cotton Gorge since 1950, and she had a homeopathic remedy for whatever ailed you. Desiree was the Queen Mother, not just of the police station, but of the whole town…and everyone knew it. If she had a dentist appointment, she could take it without having to explain.

Chili headed back for his office, and called out over his shoulder, "She left a note on your desk, though."

Ralph tossed all but two of the envelopes back on Desiree's desk. Junk mail, he figured, although he'd been wrong a couple of times and had learned to let Desiree make those decisions. In his first year in Cotton Gorge, he once received a store circular with his name on it, and had tossed it without even opening it; Desiree found it upon emptying the trash cans on her lunch break, and she absolutely shrieked at his horrible mistake. Inside the envelope was a coupon for "ten dollars off any one item of ten dollars or more" which she promptly took to the store, in the middle of her work day, and bought a truly hideous scarf which she paid, after the coupon, about fifty seven cents for; she wore that scarf (with a meaningful and perpetual glare at Ralph) every single day for a month, no matter what else her ensemble might include, in unforgiving protest of Ralph's gaffe. He never threw away junk mail after that. Nobody would.

On his desk, as Chili had said, was a handwritten note from Desiree that simply said, "Proprietor at Possum Hole needs to see you." It didn't say whether the need was urgent, or any details about what might be happening at the neighboring establishment, but Ralph glanced at the clock and figured if he went now, he'd arrive at a time when there was less of a crowd. They probably opened for lunch at eleven, and then the staff would be less available to talk, whatever they wanted to talk about.

He tossed the mail on the desk and turned back around. "I'm headed out again," he called to Chili.

"Was it something I said?" Chili asked, good-naturedly.

34

"That terrible Ligety Split joke…you knew it would cause our break-up someday."

"Dammit," Chili muttered from his office, and Ralph could still hear the smile in his voice.

It was October 6, which meant that Cotton Gorge, Louisiana was just beginning to feel the snap of autumn. The morning was almost what one might call cool…if one had never experienced the actual cool of autumn in more northerly states. Ralph zipped up the jacket he hadn't had the chance to remove yet and piled back into his French blue metallic Mercury Sable.

The drive to Possum Hole Bar and Grill felt like it took less time that the combined effort to fasten and unfasten his seatbelt. Ralph might have just walked, but it was too late to change his mind now. He pulled into the almost-empty parking lot and hopped out of his car.

A young man in an apron opened the door for him just as he reached it, and then locked it behind them. Opening wasn't for another half hour, but they had obviously been on the lookout for Detective James. "I'm not sure who I'm here to see…" Ralph began, but the aproned fellow interrupted him to say, "I'll go get Annie."

Ralph followed the young man as far as the bar, then leaned on the counter, waiting. He looked around at the décor, thinking it looked like a typical restaurant/bar: dark paneling, dark artwork, a couple of dart boards on one wall. He'd never come into this building when it was a church, so he wondered how much of this was original, and how much had been changed after Doctor Don absconded.

Just as he was taking a step towards a piece of art that looked like it might have been a child's finger painting, he heard a female voice calling his name.

"Detective James!" He turned to face the most startlingly attractive woman he had ever seen…like something out of a magazine, with the kind of red hair that didn't come from a bottle, and a figure that made the plain blue jeans and white t-shirt she was wearing look like high runway fashion. Ralph swallowed. Hard. And shook the hand that was being offered to him.

How on earth had he never seen this woman before? Why on earth had he never come to this bar before? Suddenly, he wanted very much to have lunch and dinner here every day for the rest of his life.

Determined to quickly regain his composure, Ralph internally shook off his initial reaction to the proprietress and adopted a professional air. "Ralph James," he said bluntly, though she obviously already knew that. She smiled broadly at him, and Ralph almost exhaled loudly in relief.

Her teeth were crooked. Notably crooked, and this flaw in her otherwise stunningly perfect face made him, oddly, much more comfortable.

"Annie Laurie Cherry," she said in response to his introduction. "But you can just call me Annie."

"Annie Laurie Cherry," he repeated, almost compulsively. "That's a mouthful…how'd you come by a name like that?"

"Two grandmothers and one ex-husband," she said, with a fluidity that meant she'd explained her name many, many times.

"So, Annie Laurie Cherry," Ralph grinned back at her, "what can I do for you?"

"Well, I got a weird note in yesterday's mail. I almost ignored it, but my bartender Joey kept at me till I called your office about it."

"Where is this weird note?" Ralph asked, but Annie was already turning away to go behind the bar. She ducked down where he couldn't see her for a moment, and then popped up right in front of him, causing him to startle.

"Sorry, bud," she said and smiled. Reaching across the heavy wooden counter, she handed him a single piece of paper, the kind of paper torn off of a little note pad. It was about six inches by four inches, and the handwriting on it was awkward, small, with lots of messy ink blobbing up the words. In the ambient lighting, Ralph tipped it toward the greatest source of illumination and read the words the best he could.

"The people I thought I loved, we don't think the same. There's fury in my blood, I can't stand it one more day, and I can feel that something's coming up, and I don't know what it is. But there's something dying, something being born."

Ralph turned the piece of paper over in his hands, as though looking for a signature which obviously wasn't there. "This come in an envelope?" he asked.

"Nope," Annie said. "It was in the mailbox with everything else, but that's all it was."

"Do you think this was meant for you? Or maybe for somebody else who works here? Does this message mean anything to you?"

"Sure it does!" Annie said with what sounded like surprise. "It's Barry Manilow!"

"Barry…"

"Barry Manilow. Top forty god? *Mandy*? *Can't Smile Without You*?"

Annie looked at him in disbelief as Ralph tried to make a connection to what she was saying…and then he did.

"Oh! The singer! The guy who writes the songs that make the whole world sing…right?"

Annie rolled her eyes. "Yes…and very decidedly no!" she said forcefully.

Ralph just blinked at her.

"I mean yes, Barry Manilow had a huge hit with the song *I Write the Songs*. But he didn't actually write that song. It's a whole big thing."

Ralph wanted nothing more than an excuse to listen to Annie Laurie Cherry tell him about a whole big thing.

"I guess you know this place used to be a church," she began.

"Sure. Doctor Don."

"Well, 'Doctor Don' had a big beef with Barry Manilow on account of his sister was a huge fan in her teens and Don got sick of it. So when he started his ministry" (she put air quotes around the word ministry) "he gave a series of sermons about how Barry Manilow sold his soul to the devil in exchange for worldly success, and the proof of it is all right there in the lyrics of the song *I Write the Songs*. He preached that those lyrics explain that it is actually Satan who writes all of Barry's big hit songs, and not only that, but in that song, the devil is taking credit for all of the worldly music which is clearly just a smoothly paved path to hell."

"Really?" Ralph said, impressed. "I wish I'd paid more attention to the lyrics!"

"Well, now you will. You'll never be able to unhear it. Lines like *I've been alive forever, and I wrote the very first song…*clearly Satan, right?"

"Clearly," Ralph answered seriously.

"And, *now when I look out through your eyes, I'm young again, even though I'm very old…*"

"I see what you mean. Totally Satanic stuff."

"People who are looking for evil can always find it."

"It sounds like you don't believe Barry sold his soul to the devil."

"Well, if he did, it wasn't so that he could write *that* song."

"Why not?"

"Because, like I said, Barry didn't write that song. It was written by Bruce Johnston of the Beach Boys."

"Yeah?" Ralph's eyebrows elevated by more than a centimeter.

"Yeah! Barry didn't even want to *sing* that song. He thought people would misunderstand it and think he was being egotistical. It's supposed to be poetry personifying Music itself, as though Music is a person and is describing its role in society. But Barry figured people would think he was saying that HE has been alive forever and wrote the very first song and that HE writes the songs that make the whole world sing."

"Yeah…that's what I thought."

"See?"

They just stood, looking at each other for a minute. Damn she was beautiful.

Ralph physically shook his head to break the momentary spell. "What does this have to do with your note?"

"Oh! Well. At first, I figured that a weird note with Barry Manilow lyrics was probably from someone in Doctor Don's flock…you know, someone still holding to *the truth* from the old days."

"But why would they send a note here? I mean, maybe because this used to be the church…?"

"Maybe," she said, "but more likely because…well, you know the sister whose music Doctor Don didn't like? Well, that's me." She stuck her hand out for another shake as though they were just meeting. "Annie Laurie Ward. Not my finest admission. Not something I make widely known in this little town, as you can imagine."

Ralph's eyebrows rose even higher. "You're Doctor Don's sister?"

"Yes, though the only contact we've had in many years was when I heard through our grandmother that he was in trouble…again…and I offered to buy this place from him. He needed cash pretty badly, so he sold the building and the property to me for ten grand. Only positive element he ever added to my life."

"Any chance he wrote the note himself?"

"It's unlikely. It's really not his style. I mean, he definitely goes for the outlandish, but this is over the top even for him."

Ralph picked up the piece of paper again and studied it, looking for what she might be calling "outlandish."

"I didn't see it either at first," Annie said flatly. It's the lighting in here. Like I said, I was throwing it away when Joey" (here she indicated the young man in the apron who had opened the door

40

for him earlier) "made me take it into the kitchen where it's brighter. It's written in blood."

Ralph held the note even further into the light and realized she was right. That's why it looked so messy. Blood makes a terrible ink, and it had dried to a crusty brown.

"You can keep it," Annie said, before Ralph had a chance to ask. "It isn't enough blood to think someone's life is at stake or anything. Could just be a kid's prank. But I figure it won't hurt anything for you to take a look at it."

Ralph, who had been holding the page carelessly, suddenly pinched one corner between his thumb and index finger, wishing he had an evidence bag on him. In Shreveport, he had always had an evidence bag in close proximity, but that habit had waned in his first six months of Cotton Gorge. Maybe there was an old one in the car.

"Can I call you later?" he asked, and then suddenly realized that sounded like a pickup line. "I mean…can I call you later on to tell you what I've learned about…about this?"

Annie Laurie Cherry beamed at him. "You can call me anytime, Detective James."

Ralph was grateful to get away from Annie, which was counterintuitive to his attraction to her, but he was beginning to have a problem that he didn't want her to see. He didn't want anyone to see. Detective Ralph James was beginning to have the very particular feeling behind his eyes that told him he was on the verge of desperately needing a fix.

He patted his coat pocket for the little vial that would save him, but he didn't find it. It was OK though…the thing about being an addict is that he kept his drug hidden everywhere. There was definitely a vial in the car. He flopped himself behind the steering wheel and reached to open the glovebox where relief was waiting…but then he realized that Annie may be watching him out the window. He didn't want her to see. All he needed in this little town was rumors of the local detective seen snorting his drug of choice in the parking lot of the local bar.

Just the thought set his nose tingling in anticipation. He blinked rapidly to try to keep the demon at bay until he could get himself to a private spot. Ralph drove the opposite direction from the Hogan House and pulled off in a quiet area of the Lake Zone, where he could indulge himself in peace…and then he sat there with his eyes closed until the drug took effect.

Finally feeling like himself again, he pulled back onto the road and headed for the one place where someone might be able to tell him about the bloody note on his passenger seat.

Chapter Five

It was a dark and stormy night.

And totally boring. Not a single person had checked in, and not a single person had checked out. At about nine-thirty a grubby kid had come down to the office to ask for change for the vending machine. Other than that…zip. For this, she earned $4.25 an hour.

Carmilla wrapped her coat around herself but didn't bother to button it up. She'd have to take it off the minute she got in the car. It was too bulky to drive in. The storm had died down and now only the tiniest mist of rain sparkled in the air under the streetlamp where her car was parked. With her head down, Carmilla unlocked the driver's side door, stripped off the coat and tossed it in the back, and slid into the front seat, all of this in almost one fluid motion. The car started right away, thank god, and the radio came blaring to life with a volume and intensity reflecting the happy, wakeful person Carmilla had been at noon, which was nothing like the lifeless rag which barely resembled humanity that she felt like at the end of her shift. Huey Lewis *really* wanted to do it all for his baby, and Carmilla *really* didn't want to hear about it.

She snapped the radio off violently, swearing (as she did most nights) that she would henceforth remember to turn the radio down every time she turned off the car. Not that she actually used the word "henceforth" in her internal dialogue. People who comfortably used a word like that did not work at the LaDonna Motel in Cotton Gorge, Louisiana. That was probably listed among the disqualifiers on the application.

The rain on her windshield was just enough to be troublesome. On their lowest setting, the windshield wipers were still too much, swiping away the raindrops, and then squeaking across the dry windshield in a way that made her spine tingle like the proverbial fingernails on a chalkboard. But if she turned the wipers off, her view through the windshield was obscured by rain inside twenty seconds.

Not that she used the word "obscured."

The only solution was for Carmilla to keep her hand on the wiper switch and flip it on…then off…then on…then off…all the way home. It wasn't efficient, but it kept both the rain and the spine tingles away.

In silence, Carmilla drove home in the kind of automatic daze that happens when one has driven the same path every night for eight years. She had taken the job at the LaDonna when her husband moved out, and it was supposed to just be temporary until she got on her feet again, but by now she wasn't sure she even had feet anymore. There had been a time when she believed that she would ultimately find another husband, someone who would see her for the princess her father had convinced her she was, sweep her off her feet, and vow to love, honor, cherish, and split the bills with her till death do us part. To that end, she had allowed exactly seven men into her life since her divorce.

There had been Ray, who lost his job two weeks after they started dating so he had to move in with her and six months later, still unemployed, he stole her washing machine (not the dryer, just the washer) and disappeared on a Tuesday.

Next was Stephen, who lost his job two *days* after they started dating, so he had to move in with her and eight months later, still unemployed, he made the mistake of letting his *new* girlfriend stay overly long following an afternoon tryst, so that Carmilla caught them together when she got home from the LaDonna.

Next was Burt, who wasn't employed when they met, though he talked a big game about prospects. He moved in with her to be closer to a potential job, but when that fell through he seemed to take up permanent residence in her living room recliner, until the Sunday when he slapped her for suggesting he might get up and get his own beer this time.

Almost anyone could look at this list and see the developing pattern, which continued with very little variation throughout the entire list of seven. Almost anyone except Carmilla. Rather than recognizing that her M.O. of seeking each new partner from the clientele of the same honky-tonk dive might lead to the same relationship experience over and over, Carmilla just felt truly victimized. She carried the oppression of every one of those failures like a heavy blanket that threatened to smother her in the silence of a dark and stormy night. She flipped the wipers off again…then on again…and sighed under the weight of it.

Carmilla's little house was on the outside edge of town, right on the line where the houses stopped and the farms began. It had been her parents' house, and when they were gone it just naturally became hers. She had never even changed the décor, as it still felt like their place. She would go in tonight, like every other night, and fix herself a little something in the microwave her Mom had been so proud of when she bought it new, then sit down in front of the little color television her Dad had been so proud of when he bought it new. If the air was just right, she could get KTBS channel 3 out of Shreveport, and she could watch the late movie and fall asleep in her chair, the same chair her father, her ex-husband, and seven deadbeat boyfriends had fallen asleep in, before finally rousing and dragging herself down the hallway, lined with faded elementary school pictures of herself, displayed in cheap gold leaf 8x10 frames from TG&Y, to the bedroom where she would crash until tomorrow when she would do it all again.

The one helpful thing Ray had done—or was it Stephen?—before moving out was to install an automatic garage door opener so that Carmilla no longer had to get out of her car and open the garage by hand before getting back in the car, driving in, getting out of the car again and closing the door by hand. Of course, Ray, or whoever it was, hadn't done this to save Carmilla the trouble, only to save himself the trouble...but Carmilla was the ultimate beneficiary.

On a night like this, with the sky still spitting on her, she was particularly thankful for the remote control that she had attached to the dash with a little strip of Velcro.

Carmilla eased her Datsun into the garage, even as the door graciously lifted to allow her. Before the door was all the way up, she pushed the other button on the remote so that the door jolted itself into reverse motion, slowly groaning to a close behind her. Shutting off the engine, she stepped out into the foul-smelling garage and up the two steps to her kitchen door.

Inside, she flipped on the light switch and tossed her keys on the counter by the sink. From the freezer, she chose a Swanson "Classic Fried Chicken Dinner" and tossed it in the microwave without even reading the instructions. They always said "open this part and stir this part, remove that thing and then cook at half power for three minutes, then pull back the cover and spoon the gravy and replace the thing you took out before and then cover it with something new and then cook at full power for another three minutes." Geez...for all that trouble she could go kill a chicken, pluck it, chop it, batter it, and fry it up herself. She had long ago learned that five minutes in the microwave was good enough for anything.

With her hand in an oven mitt and her dinner balanced on the mitt, Carmilla strolled to the living room, where she promptly dropped it on the floor and Swanson Classic Fried Chicken splattered all over her mother's braid rug. Standing in the living room, blocking

46

the front door, was an elderly woman in a pink button-up housedress brandishing a…what was it? Was that a *sword*?

There was no time to study on the matter. In the half light of the living room, which was only illuminated by the light coming from the kitchen, the old woman began literally hissing…like a snake…and then she said, in a low, horrible voice, "You vermin are all alike. You just take whatever you want!" Then the old lady took a step forward and Carmilla turned to run.

Back the way she came was the only escape. There were two doors in Carmilla's house: the front door out of the living room, which the old lady with the sword was blocking, and the kitchen door into the garage. But the second Carmilla got into the garage, she realized her horrible mistake. The garage door opener was there, on its little strip of Velcro, right where she could see it through the windshield…but her car was locked. And her keys were on the counter by the sink. And the little old lady was coming down the steps.

"Slow down!" she hissed as she raised her weapon in the darkness of the garage, "*You're shaking the fish!*"

Carmilla had the strangest thought in that moment. She recalled simultaneously two lines of lyric from *Hotel California*, the line about "we are all just prisoners here, of our own device" and the other line that said "you can check out any time you like, but you can never leave." She had incarcerated herself in her parents' garage—in her own garage—and now death was raining down upon her.

Of course, in her inner dialogue, she didn't use the word "incarcerated."

Chapter Six

"Well, this is friggin' weird stuff, but I don't think it's evidence of a crime."

"Oh no?"

"No. I mean, it's blood all right…but it isn't human."

The coroner held the offending Barry Manilow lyrics in one hand and wiped his other on his lab coat.

"Not human? Then what is it?" Ralph asked, scratching his head in perplexity.

"Can't really tell…some kind of animal. It's not even enough blood to be worried what happened to the critter. A note like this could have been written with less than a vial of blood like a vet might draw to do a liver panel before a simple spay or neuter. My guess is the author used something like a toothpick as a sort of fountain pen, dipping the tip in the blood every couple of letters or so till it was all spelled out."

Mike Dissart had been the coroner serving Cotton Gorge, as well as several other surrounding small towns, since he and his wife Becky had moved there in 1979. The fun story was that he had been the President of the Fort Worth chapter of the Sonny and Cher fan club, and Becky had been his Vice President. That's how they met. They married right out of high school, combined their fanship through college, then Mike went on to medical school while Becky stayed home to raise the babies.

Ralph figured that Mike saw the world the same way he did…that a medical professional in Fort Worth was a needle in a big pile of needles, but the same man in Cotton Gorge was the whole haystack.

In the big city, Mike might have spent his days working more high-profile cases: grisly murders, crime spree evidence, gang violence victims, big public court testimonies. In Cotton Gorge, this toothpick note in a thimble's-worth of animal blood was an interesting break from death by natural causes, the occasional slip-and-fall, and perhaps a terrible farm machinery or hunting accident every couple of years or so.

"I could send it off to a lab in Dallas," Mike was saying. "It would probably cost a thousand dollars and take at least a month to get results. Seems unnecessary to me. I kinda figure somebody wanted to scare somebody, so they did this crazy thing. But it looks like nobody was hurt, on either end of the note, so I wouldn't bother with the lab if I was you."

Mike handed the note back to Ralph, who slipped it back into the evidence bag. "So that's a dead end then, I suppose."

"I suppose."

Ralph was just turning to go back to the station, but Mike's assistant Rusty stepped through the swinging door into the exam room. "Phone call, Mike."

Mike waved it away with a smile. "Take a message. I just need to scrub up."

"No," said Rusty, not smiling. "You're gonna wanna take this one. There's been a murder."

Mike headed for the phone in the outer office, but in the end he didn't take the call. Ralph did.

"This is Detective James," he said gruffly into the phone.

"Ralph?" he heard Desiree's voice on the other end of the line.

"Desi…what's up?"

"It's bad Ralph. There's been a dead woman found in the dumpster behind the Pack a Sack."

"Is Chili already there?"

"Probably not yet. He left just as I was dialing Mike's number."

"Anybody say who the woman is?"

"No…" Desiree paused. "I think they can't tell. It sounds pretty bad."

Ralph hung up the phone without any peasantries. Desi didn't expect them.

Without need of invitation, Mike hopped in the passenger side of Ralph's Sable and they rode wordlessly to the Pack a Sack. The front store window was almost entirely covered with a picture of an enormous smiling cartoon camel, looking like he was just *so* excited to get people to start smoking at least three packs a day. Ralph took a right turn at the entrance and wound his way to the back of the little building where six or seven people were gathered like opportunistic house flies by the big green dumpster. Chili came running around from the other side of the building, and immediately began shooing the flies away.

"Come on now…you know you can't be here," he said cajolingly to the little crowd of looky-loos. "Y'all go on home now. You'll see it all on the news."

Taking some of them physically by the shoulders, Chili guided the group back around the building the way he had just come, leaving Ralph and Mike alone with Drew Marshall, the manager of the Pack a Sack.

"I was just throwing out the trash," Drew said softly, his eyes lowered, "and I saw her in there. I don't usually even look in. I usually just throw the bags over the top and walk away. Don't know why I did it different this time. I just did."

Ralph patted Drew on the arm and then stepped forward to lean over the opening of the dumpster. He didn't take more than two seconds' glance before backing away and calling for Mike.

Mike stepped forward as well. Slightly more accustomed to a sight like this, Mike was able to stand on tiptoe for almost a whole minute taking in the scene. By the time he stepped back, Chili had returned to join them.

Mike shook his head. "Damn," he said. "That's the most awful thing I've ever seen."

Ralph nodded somberly. "Looks like she was stabbed about five hundred times." Gathering his composure, Ralph stepped forward again, and this time he and Mike both peered over into the dumpster.

"I don't see how y'all can do that," Chili remarked. "That dumpster smells like hell. Smells like a whole family of orangutans caught syphilis and hid in there to die. On a hot day. And I don't mean because of *her*. I mean because...damn, Drew!...what are you throwing away in there? Smells like hell for Thanksgiving."

Ralph ignored Chili's complaints. The smell didn't bother him. It was one of the benefits of long-term drug abuse. His sense of smell was almost completely gone.

"I don't think that's stab wounds, Ralph," Mike said at last. "Too shallow. It looks more like a gang of thugs attacked her with a series of kitchen slice-and-dice tools. It's just a million shallow cuts all over. She died from exsanguination, but not from any of the wounds themselves. There's just so many of the buggers she bled out."

"I don't know how y'all can do that," Chili began again. "Just standin there breathin that mess. Smells like a leprous llama climbed in there and tried to make Sun Tea with his own intestines."

"I guess we'll have to try to identify her by her teeth. Can't see any of her facial features at all. Man, I've never seen a job like this. Not even when Randy Miller got caught in his own thresher. That was bad, but at least I could still tell it was Randy. This is…man, this is awful. Is she an out of towner, do you reckon?"

Ralph was silent for a moment, then sighing, he said, "No." He pointed to the mutilated right arm which was stretched out over the garbage, as though reaching for the crumpled box of Nature Valley Crunchy Granola Bars. Indicating the tacky lime green press-on fingernails, he said, "I've met her. Night clerk at the LaDonna. Carmen or…Caramel…something."

Mike used Drew's phone to call his team to come with a van, while Chili took snapshots of the scene and Ralph wrote down everything he could see that might be evidence. That wasn't much. The dumpster sat on one end of a large asphalt parking lot, where a dozen cars parked every day. A hundred footsteps made by scores of people, none of them leaving a detectable or outstanding trace or track. If indeed a gang of kitchen-knife hackers had come here in the night to dump their victim, Ralph wouldn't be able to discern that from any of the other people who came and went from this parking lot in the course of their daily errands.

When Mike returned, followed by two burly fellows with a gurney, Ralph and Chili cleared out. They rode in silence back to

Hogan House, each musing on the purpose of existence, the nature of mortality. Thankfully, like life, it was a short ride.

Desiree looked up with interest when they opened the door. "Well?" she queried.

Stomping his boots on the mat, Ralph answered, "It's as bad as you think. Probably worse. Mike's taking her back to his place for a real exam."

"Is it someone we know?" Desiree almost whispered.

"It's the girl who was the night clerk at the LaDonna. I can't remember her name. I'll go down there in a little while and ask some questions."

Desiree's hands flew to her face in horror. "Carmilla!" she gasped. "Carmilla Rabbi!"

"You knew her?"

"All her life! Her Mama was a friend of mine. Fine people. Carmilla used to take piano lessons from my sister. Sweet girl. Not too bright, but a good girl."

Ralph put his hand on Desi's shoulder as he passed her desk. What could he say?

He had just sat down at his desk and put his head in his hands when Chili came wandering in. "This is just unbelievable. I can't even remember when we had a murder in Cotton Gorge. I thought Earl Pickens was gonna shoot his wife that night she kicked his Rottweiler for eating the chicken she had put on the counter to thaw…but he didn't." Chili's voice softened. "I went to high school with Carmilla. I didn't really know her, but I always saw her around."

He was silent for a moment, contemplating, then he moved back into more comfortable conversational territory.

"I may never get that stench out of my nose, though! Smells like it's stuck up there forever. I'll have to dig the goo out of a Glade Push-up and smear it in my nostrils. That thing smelled like a rotting tuna fell in love with an elephant's pancreas and they went in there to raise their toxic offspring. Man, I don't know how y'all stood it."

Looking up at last, Ralph snapped, "Chili, go to your own office to write your Doctoral Dissertation on *How Bad the Dumpster Behind the Pack a Sack Smells*! Write it and then get over it, because you're the rung on the ladder that's going to get in that dumpster and take everything out looking for any further evidence."

Chili looked genuinely shocked. "Like what? Suspicious banana peels and stale coffee grounds?"

"Like the murder weapons," Ralph retorted. "Once the body is gone, go back and go over everything in the dumpster, and bag up anything that doesn't belong there."

"It's a dumpster for gods sake!" Chili protested. "Nothing belongs there...or everything belongs there! How can anyone tell the difference?"

"Out Chili!" Ralph said through gritted teeth. "And close the door."

Ralph's frustration was only partly based in Chili's insistence on a string of similes for the dumpster aroma. Mostly he needed privacy to tend to his addiction. It had been nearly eight hours, and he tried not to ever go past six. He knew he needed to quit. He had become a slave to the drug, and he always told himself that the time would come when he would sincerely devote himself to detox and recovery...but that time couldn't be today. Today, for the first time since he became a detective, he had a murder to solve.

Chapter Seven

Annie Laurie Ward always hated those get-to-know-you games at school where kids were asked to tell something interesting or unknown about themselves. Other kids got to share answers like, "I saw Star Wars eleven times!" or "My grandpa has a Beta Max!" or "We went to Yellowstone last summer!"

The overarching "interesting and unknown" thing about Annie Laurie Ward is that she was raised in a religious cult. And because she knew how *very* interesting this would be to her peers, she was determined to keep it "unknown."

Annie Laurie had come to understand, at some point in her teens, that the word "cult" could be easily defined as *any small religion that you're not part of.* Like all other cults, her cult did not identify itself as a cult...but what cult ever did? She came to understand that her particular cult checked all the boxes for cult criteria, according to a book she found on her grandmother's shelf. Her grandmother (the Laurie part of her name) had not been at all pleased when Annie's parents had decided on this path, but the main thing about joining a cult is that it is really hard to change your mind.

Among its other methods for staying utterly separate from mainstream religion (things like not allowing Christmas or Easter or Halloween or birthday celebrations, all the things that made the other children in Hattiesburg Mississippi happy), this cult also had its own hymnal of weird songs, mostly taken directly from scriptures about slaying one's enemies and the Lord smiting those that oppose His flock. But one song stood out to Annie as she matured: the one that quoted I Corinthians 1:26, "Not many wise men now are called, not many noble brethren, not many mighty chosen ones..."

As a child, the cult was Annie's whole world. Her friends, her activity center. Sitting primly through four hours of sermons every Saturday were just the dues she paid for the rest of it, and the rest of it seemed fine. But as she grew into her teens, that song about the "not many wise men" began to niggle at her. She began to look around at these people she knew so well—the only people she was allowed to have a social life with—and realized that these were the *not wise men* who had been called into this "church." These desperately poor, almost wholly uneducated people who were being promised that they would be the Kings and Priests in the coming World Tomorrow that God was bringing in these, the prophesied end times…they were not wise men, for sure. Not noble or mighty.

The only mighty ones were the cult leaders. They had enormous power over the lives of these poor people, and they were paid handsomely. The church exacted thirty percent in tithes from their followers, and the followers paid it because the alternative—to be put out of the body of the church into outer darkness—was far worse than living in poverty. Conversely the reward—to be a King over all the unwashed masses of worldly people for a millennium—was far better than any full belly or reasonable housing situation for your family in *this* life.

At least that's what the cult (quite successfully) convinced its followers.

When Annie Laurie was a senior in high school, she met Dave Cherry, a senior himself, and a fellow who had never heard of her cult. Dave only saw her as a pretty redhead with a wicked sense of humor. Annie saw Dave as a lifeline. On the night before graduation, Annie Laurie and Dave eloped to the next county, and when she announced this to her parents after the pomp and circumstance, she was summarily cut off from the cult.

This had rather been the goal.

Annie's marriage to Dave was a wild ride that lasted 249 days, during which time they had lived entirely in his big land yacht Oldsmobile. They still kept in Christmas card contact, and once or twice a year they chatted on the phone for an hour or so. She kept his name because it represented her freedom from the cult, and because she still loved him dearly…just not as a husband. Ever since the day of her shameful "disfellowshipment" from the Body, Annie Laurie had been reveling in her freedom to be who she wanted, do what she wanted. Owning a bar and grill would definitely not be an approvable career choice for a woman in her previous life, and that's part of why she loved it so much.

Growing up in a cult had quite a different effect on Annie's little brother Donny. Donny Ward didn't bother looking around at all the not wise men in the congregation; his eyes were on the ministry. Sitting there in his hand-me-down suit, he studied the men who got to keep the money that his family had to give. These men lived in nice houses, wore new clothes, drove shiny new cars. These men had absolute power over their followers. Donny wanted all of that.

Annie had a vivid memory of the first time her little brother had been deemed old enough to sit through a church service rather than stay in the nursery with the toddlers. Donny was sitting between Annie and their mother when the offering basket was passed down the row. When Annie dutifully handed the basket to Donny, he held it for a moment, staring at the pile of dollar bills and shiny coins, and he said, "Do I put some in…or take some out?"

Becoming the one who got to "take some out" was Donny Ward's ultimate goal.

Donny stayed with his parents in the cult for two years after Annie Laurie separated herself from the family. At nineteen, he moved from Hattiesburg to Columbia where he spent all of his high school odd-job savings to rent an empty building that had once been a Dollar General, and to print up a hundred flyers advertising his new church. In Columbia, they had never seen such a fired up young man, and the newly christened Doctor Don attracted a wide swathe of the county with his services which included (beyond the fiery Sunday sermons) weddings, couples and family counseling, anointing and healing, and exorcism. Each of these services came at the price of fifteen to fifty dollars, and absolute loyalty to Doctor Don.

The washing clean of his flock from all stains of Barry Manilow was free.

Once forcibly emancipated from the cult, Annie Laurie was no longer allowed contact with her parents, so her only news of her family now came through her grandmother. Through Grandma Laurie, she learned about Donny's transformation in Doctor Don, and then about his brief time in county lock up, and then—later—about his similar story in Cotton Gorge. By that time, Annie had finished a business degree at a community college in Jackson, and she contacted Donny about buying him out.

Starting over in Cotton Gorge had been pleasant for Annie. Before she opened the Possum Hole, there had only been one bar in town—the one where Carmilla had met all of her exes—and they didn't serve food. She very quickly built a regular list of customers, and rarely had what they might call "a slow night." Her first hire had been Joey Morouse, who she trained to be a bartender, a trick she had learned during her 249 days as Mrs. Dave Cherry.

Joey was more than an employee to Annie; he was a good friend. At nineteen, he was only six years her junior, but she felt an absolutely maternal sense of protectiveness for him. He responded by always asking her opinion on his ideas, his wardrobe, his schedule, and his girlfriends. That last one was really important. If Joey was interested in a girl and Annie Laurie didn't like her...his interest waned.

So, on the Monday that the blood-stained note arrived in the mailbox at the Possum Hole, Joey wasn't going to let Annie Laurie pass it off as harmless. Anyone who takes the time to write a note in blood is not harmless. Besides insisting that she call the police to report it, Joey immediately began escorting Annie home every night and going in before her to check out no one else was in the place.

Annie Laurie felt like all of this was unnecessary, but she loved that it mattered to Joey.

When the Wednesday night crowd came into the Possum Hole talking about the body of Carmilla Rabbi being found in the dumpster behind the Pack a Sack, Joey stubbornly insisted that he'd been right, and Annie was in danger. Annie, on the other hand, assured him that there was no connection. Rumor had it that Carmilla had been recently dating a fellow from Houghton who had been drummed out of the Army for domestic violence, and it looked like he had now taken that penchant out on Carmilla.

Between the entirely fabricated story of the dishonorably discharged murderer, and the almost equally fabricated descriptions of the condition of the body, all the discussion at the Possum Hole that night were about Carmilla. Pity…she had never been so interesting or popular in life, but now everyone in town claimed some kind of connection or friendship or kinship.

"I been knowing that girl all my life," Annie overheard one woman say. "We was best friends in eighth grade. I tell you, nobody could part us. Course in later years I ain't seen too much of her, but we still woulda been best friends even so."

"Well, you wouldn'ta wanted to see her today," the man she was talking to retorted. "The way I hear tell, her eyeballs was cut out and stuffed into the holes where her ears used to be. Leastwise that's what Bobby Corbett told me, and he heard it from Larry Shanklin and Larry saw it for himself!"

By Drunk Hour, which was 11pm, the time all the previously happy glowing customers were beginning to feel the natural depressant effect of the alcohol, Annie Laurie heard no less than three different men telling Joey that they had been secretly in love with Carmilla, and didn't know how they would get over it. Joey listened with the trained empathy of a bartender but did not fall prey to the obvious ploy that each of these men was hoping to drink on the house on account of their terrible loss and the lifetime of crippling regret to come.

When the bar closed at one AM, Joey and Annie had each heard a hundred stories of Carmilla's amazing life and how deeply adored she was by the town. Apparently, she had been secretly supporting the local animal shelter by giving half her paycheck to that organization for years. On her days off, she visited widows. In her free time, she knitted sweaters for orphans in Mexico, and once Debbie Palmer had seen her, clear as day, taking off her own coat and using it to cover up a man sleeping on a park bench, because that's just the kind of person she was.

Next stop: sainthood.

It was only a pity Carmilla never knew any of these things about herself.

"You're not going to believe the till tonight," Joey called to Annie as she locked the door behind the final customer.

"Really? Is it good?"

"I haven't done an official count yet, but I'd guess it's the best night we've had since last year when Jim Breakfield decided to test drive his new Mastercard and wound up maxing it out buying rounds for the whole house."

"Really?" Annie asked, surprised. "That good?"

"I guess nothing like a true tragedy to jack up people's bar tabs."

"I guess." Annie said. "But don't count it all now. Let's lock up and take care of all that in the morning. The cash register isn't going anywhere in the next few hours, and I know you've gotta be exhausted."

"I could sleep," Joey agreed, shutting the door with a loud scrape followed by a ding. "Let me get my coat and I'll follow you home."

"You don't need you to do that, Joey. You know I'll be fine. Nobody in this town wants to hurt me…if they did, they'd lose the bar!"

"I'm coming with you whether you like it or not. The note was bad enough, now this murder. If it was broad daylight, I'd feel different, but it's one-thirty in the morning, and I'm following you home."

Annie Laurie smiled quietly to herself. It was nice to be worried about…to a point. But how long could this go on? The writer of the note may never be revealed, and what if the murderer was just someone passing through? Someone who didn't like the room service at the LaDonna? How long would the crime go unsolved before Joey gave up and let her go home by herself?

She ducked into her office for her keys and when she returned, Joey was already standing at the door, holding it open just a crack to keep the cold out. He pushed up his sleeve to check his watch and Annie laughed at him.

"Isn't that the watch Darla gave you? I thought you hated that thing…it's like the size for a sixth-grade girl!"

"Yeah, well…it's the only watch I have right now with a working battery. I keep meaning to go get new batteries in some other watches, but I don't know. Never seems to be time, or if there is, I don't remember to do it."

"Some other watches?" Annie grinned as she let Joey open the door for her. "How many do you have?"

"I don't know…a dozen maybe. That seems to be every girl's favorite present for Christmas or birthday or whatever. I just keep saying thank you and putting them in the drawer."

Annie realized that with a face like Joey's, he was probably going to collect a couple hundred more watches over the years. Those almost-black curls, green eyes and baby soft skin with just enough beard shadow to show he was a man…he was too pretty for most girls to pass up. She was glad he seemed to be choosy. She didn't want to see him get caught up and heartbroken.

As Annie pulled her little Honda out of the Possum Hole parking lot, Joey fired up his truck and followed her. When they got to her place, he got out and went to the door, where she unlocked it for him and waited on the stoop until he had gone through, turning on all the lights and checking every room. At last, he came back to the door and welcomed her inside with a sweeping motion of his arm, like a king's footman inviting a courtier into the throne room.

"Thanks for being my knight in shining t-shirt," she said as he ducked back into the chilly night air.

"Thanks for being my damsel in distress…every knight needs one to define him. I'll see you tomorrow!"

Annie closed the door behind him and took a deep breath. What a night this had been! The Possum Hole had been so busy, she'd hardly had time to even process the news of the murder. It must have been terrible. The images in her mind were based on the gory details shared by her customers, and while none of the stories matched, all of them were equally graphic and grisly.

She supposed Detective James would not be calling her about the note any time soon now that he had something much more pressing to deal with. She had to acknowledge a selfish pang of regret, as though Carmilla had inconvenienced her.

Annie shook it off.

Hanging her keys on the hook by the door, she went to the kitchen for a bedtime snack. She knew it was terrible to eat so late, but in all the busy of the evening, she hadn't stopped to fix herself dinner, and she was self-aware enough to know that an empty belly would keep her awake and then she'd be worthless tomorrow. Standing in front of an open fridge, she scanned the contents and decided on a Tupperware container of leftover rice and veggies. Somehow, it seemed less like a midnight meal if she didn't heat it up, so she just tossed the lid in the sink and grabbed a fork.

Eating as she walked, Annie wandered down the short hallway to her bedroom. The lights were all still on from Joey's inspection, so she flipped them each off as she passed. Kitchen, living room, hallway…all dark now. In the bedroom, she turned on the bedside lamp before turning off the overhead. In between bites of cold leftovers, she changed into her pajamas, washed her face and brushed out her thick auburn hair. When the Tupperware was empty, she brushed her teeth and then climbed into bed. Reaching for the novel on her nightstand, Annie paused.

What was *that*?

She listened intently in the silence and thought she heard it again...the softest sound. She couldn't tell if it was just outside or...*or in the house.*

Absolutely frozen, Annie listened to see if she heard it again, but all she could hear was the vortex of blood pressure throbbing in her own ears. She wasn't given to paranoia. She was long accustomed to living alone. But in that moment, her thoughts were crowded with Joey's warnings and the imagined pictures of Carmilla Rabbi's mutilated body, and Barry Manilow's lyrics "something's coming up and I don't know what it is, but there's something dying...something being born."

The momentary paralysis passed as suddenly as it had taken hold, and Annie threw back the covers and leapt from her bed. In perfect reverse order, she turned back on every light in the house as she made her way back to the living room. The house was empty.

And then she heard it again. It was definitely outside. It sounded like it was coming from the porch.

Without considering that she might be safer behind the locked front door, Annie threw it open and looked out into the night. Her eyes fought to adjust to the darkness, before she thought to flip on the porch light. At first, she had a moment of confusion because she could see that Joey's truck was still parked behind her car, and that made no sense to her. But then she heard the sound again, right at her feet, and she looked down.

Even in the glare of the porch light, Annie had to bend over and peer at the form to try to understand what she was seeing. There was so much blood, on everything. On the porch, on the lump of flesh, soaked through what remained of the clothes the lump of flesh was kind of still wearing. Everything was ripped up, ripped apart. From head to toe, this hulk was unrecognizable as human, much less as anyone that she might know…until she glanced at what had been the left arm and saw the sixth-grade-girl sized watch that was still ticking away. The only sign of life.

Chapter 8

What a person generally does not want is to be out at four o'clock in the morning when a person really needs to be sleeping. But when a person has no choice but to be out at four o'clock in the morning, that person definitely doesn't want to be spending that time under the harsh fluorescent lights of the morgue.

But on this early Thursday morning, which still felt like Wednesday since he hadn't been to bed yet, the morgue was exactly where Ralph James had to be. Well, maybe he didn't have to be here, but he didn't feel right leaving Mike to manage this by himself, and besides, Mike might come up with something that would need his help.

Laid out on the cold steel table, the body of Carmilla Rabbi looked slightly more human than it had in the dumpster. At least now he could see the basic shape of head, torso, arms, legs. The frizzled red hair was matted with dried blood; the face, which he could barely recall from their brief encounter, was obliterated by the scores of small slashes.

With the help of his assistant, Mike had gotten Carmilla cleaned up. The wounds were no longer bleeding, so now they could be more forensically observed. Ralph felt again a wave of pity for Carmilla, lying there naked on the cold table. What a way to go.

As the number continued to rise, Mike had begun counting aloud, at first in a whisper, and then a little louder, until finally his voice was practically echoing off the sterile walls.

"Seven hundred twenty-three, seven hundred twenty-four, seven hundred twenty-five, twenty-six, twenty-seven, twenty-eight! Seven hundred twenty-eight! I think I got them all."

Ralph just whistled low at the magnitude of that final number.

"Of course that's hardly official. I figure I probably double counted some and missed counting others…but that's close enough." Mike removed his gloves and sighed heavily as he tossed them into the biohazard can across the room.

"Any new thoughts on how this happened?" Ralph asked, trying not to yawn.

It had indeed been a very long day for Mike and Ralph. Once they had gotten Carmilla's body back to the lab, they went together to her house, where the found the scene of the crime in her closed garage. Carmilla's blood was splattered everywhere, and the hood and driver's side of her Datsun were scratched up in a similar pattern to the shallow cuts all over her body.

After thoroughly examining and photographing the murder scene, they had gone together to the LaDonna to talk to the manager, Eric Petty, about his long-time employee. Eric assured them that everyone had liked Carmilla.

"Well," he corrected himself sheepishly, "I guess what I mean is that nobody *didn't* like her."

"Can you clarify?" Ralph asked, looking up from his notes.

"I mean…Carmilla wasn't the kind of girl people *didn't* like, but I guess people didn't really like her either. She didn't…make much of an impression. She did her job; I could always count on her to show up when she was supposed to. She didn't complain, but she also didn't smile. I hate to say it, but that's why I always kept her on the night shift. The day people need to be friendly like. Personable. They need to be able to listen to people tell their stories and chat with them, make them feel welcome at the LaDonna. Carmilla just wasn't interested in any of that.

"I tried to tell her. I mean, I felt bad leaving her on the night shift when she was my senior employee. You know, most people I hire stay for a year, maybe two. It's not a long-term career choice. But Carmilla, she just became a fixture; eight years she worked here. Several times I told her she could have the day shift if she would try a little harder to be friendly, to talk to people like she cared…but she didn't. I mean she didn't talk to them. I don't know if she cared."

"But you're not aware of any kind of altercation with anyone? She didn't shortchange somebody, or give them the wrong room…walk in on them in the shower? Anything like that?" Ralph imagined motel staff had all kinds of access to things the customers wouldn't like.

"Well, there was one time when she went to help clean up a room from a late check out and there was a giant spider in the bathroom, and Carmilla…well, you gotta figure most folks would do the same…but she just stomped on it and squealed. But then the guest came back in about an hour carrying a little plastic aquarium and saying how his pet tarantula had gotten loose and could he please go back into the room to get it. He was pretty upset when he found out what happened. He didn't know how Carmilla couldn't tell a pet giant fuzzy spider from any regular old giant fuzzy spider. That was bad. He got me involved, almost got you involved. I paid him four hundred bucks to calm down. Carmilla felt pretty bad, but it wasn't her fault. She offered to let me take the four hundred out of her wages over time, but I said no. I'd have squished the thing myself."

"Do you have this fella's information?"

"Oh, sure. It's in the records. But that was about three years ago."

Ralph stopped writing. Three years ago. It was highly doubtful anyone had been nursing a grievance over a dead spider for that long.

Sitting in the morgue at four AM, Ralph could only acknowledge again that this had to have been done by more than one person. The seven hundred twenty-eight cuts were all over her body, at every angle. A single person would have had to physically roll the already lifeless body over on the floor to continue making that many cuts. That kind of overkill just seemed unlikely.

But then a gang, even if every member were armed with exactly the same kind of kitchen slice-and-dice tool that Mike had suggested earlier, would have still produced different kinds of wounds depending on the strength and intensity of the strikes of each individual member. But Carmilla's wounds all had a remarkable *same*ness that would indicate a level of gang organization that also seemed unlikely.

As a beat cop in Shreveport, Ralph had worked quite a few gang violence cases, but in Cotton Gorge, the closest thing to gang activity was the group of local teenagers playing tag in Woodson McGuffee's corn. Ralph knew every one of those kids and suspected none of them of greater malfeasance than raising Woodson's blood pressure with their antics…and that wasn't hard to do.

But even in Shreveport, where gang activity was rampant and he had seen plenty of the aftermath of their violence, he'd never seen anything like this. What had happened to Carmilla just didn't even make any sense. How could anyone attack with both that level of rage and that level of fastidiousness?

Mike broke through Ralph's musing with a soft little "Hmmm…"

"What is it?" Ralph asked.

Wearing fresh gloves, Mike had been going over Carmilla's body again, and was now holding something up to the light, pinched in a pair of tweezers. "Looks like…hay. Like a tiny piece of hay. It was inside one of the cuts on her abdomen."

Ralph stood up and stepped over to take a look. In a farm town, hay was as common as power outages. It was usual, almost expected, to see someone all dressed up in their Sunday best, who still had a little piece of hay stuck to their back or dragging on their shoe…but generally not *inside* their body.

"How do you reckon it got there?" Ralph queried. "Was she maybe dragged at some point?"

"No…there is no other evidence of her being dragged. Did you notice if there was any hay in her garage? Like maybe she flopped around on the floor while…you know…while this was all happening?"

"I can look over the photos once we get them developed, but I didn't notice it. Of course, I almost don't notice hay. There's hay everywhere. There's probably hay in here."

"There is," Mike said, raising the tweezers. "Right here."

"That's not what I…"

When one is unavoidably spending the four o'clock hour in the harsh fluorescent lights of the morgue, one does not expect to hear the phone ring.

"It will ring through to the service," Mike assured him, but even so, both men stepped to the swinging doors and each held one open to listen. When the machine picked up, they heard Desiree Ligety's voice on the other end.

"Mike? Ralph? Are either of you there?"

By the time she said "there" both men had rushed to the phone and Ralph picked it up.

"Desi. You OK?"

"I'm fine, Ralph…a little shaken just because I was asleep when the call came. Ralph…there's been another one."

Together, both men groaned, "Oh no…"

"Where?" Ralph asked, already clutching the keys in his jeans pocket.

"Well, that's the thing. This one is apparently alive, at least for now. They've taken him to the DeSoto Parish Hospital. By the time Chili got the call—and then called me—the victim was already there. I don't know anything else. I knew you'd want to hear right away."

"Thanks, Desi. I'm on it. You can go back to sleep."

"I can assure you that's not going to happen."

Mike stayed behind to get Carmilla tucked in for the night, and Ralph headed out into the cold pre-dawn. Cotton Gorge had a tiny clinic and a single doctor, but for a hospital, local residents had to go to the DeSoto Parish Hospital in Mansfield. It was a thirty-five-minute drive on a long dark road with nothing to look at but the pool of headlights in front of his car, and Ralph had time to think.

Two murders in two days. Apparently, gang violence in a small town where everyone knew everyone and no gangs had been seen. Was this new victim in any way connected to Carmilla? Was it a friend or relative who might have been involved in something that he had overlooked in Carmilla's life? Or would this be another woman of the same basic age and type? Desi had said "he" …but maybe she was just guessing. People tended to speak in the masculine when they really meant either/or. Did Desi do that? He couldn't remember.

He thought back to that day in the motel lobby with Carmilla. She had flirted with him a little, he thought. Or she was trying to. She wasn't very good at it. Why was he only ever flirted with by women he didn't want to be flirting with him? He could picture her quite clearly just then, the way her eyes wrinkled up when she smiled at him that way, and then through the softly falling snowflakes, he saw her wrinkles all begin to split open and bleed, all over her face, her eyes running with tears of thick dark blood.

Ralph jolted awake and nearly swerved off the road. Maybe he should have brought Mike along after all, just to keep him from falling asleep at the wheel. He shook his head and slapped himself twice on each cheek. It wasn't snowing, Carmilla was still back in Mike's lab, and Ralph was, at last, pulling into the ER parking lot of the DeSoto Parish Hospital.

Hurrying to the registration window, Ralph flashed his badge and explained why he was here. The receptionist called a nurse who ushered Detective James out of the ER and into the main hospital, hurrying down the hall to the ICU where, Ralph was shocked to find, he was greeted by Annie Laurie Cherry.

He could tell immediately that she hadn't slept either; but more than that, he could tell she had been crying. A lot.

"Detective James," she breathed as she approached him.

"What is it, Annie…are you hurt?"

"No. No. I'm fine. I mean…no, I'm not fine."

Hearing the tears threatening her voice, Ralph placed a calming hand on Annie's shoulder. She looked up at him.

"It's Joey. My Joey…I mean, my bartender. You met him yesterday…the other day. God, I don't even know what day it is."

"Take your time," Ralph said. "Let's go find a place to sit and you can tell me."

The waiting area for the ICU was empty at this hour, except for one elderly fellow reading a back issue of *Highlights* magazine in the far corner. Annie Laurie laughed and said, "My parents used to order that magazine for my brother and me. I remember once we got an issue that Donny loved so much, he wanted to sleep with it, and then he wet the bed. Totally ruined the magazine. He was so upset…and he was really too old to be wetting the bed…"

What had begun as a funny story broke off at the end into a choked sob. Annie put her head in her hands and Ralph helped her lower into a chair.

"It was so terrible," she said, finally looking up at him. "Joey has been really worried about me, and he followed me home to make sure there weren't any monsters waiting for me. Then he said goodnight and I just went about my business. Stupid stuff…fixing food and changing clothes, brushing my teeth…and all the time, just outside, he was…he was…"

Ralph didn't push her. She would tell him.

"What if the killer had come for me?" she said forcefully. "What if it was supposed to be me, but I locked myself up all cozy and Joey got it instead?"

"Don't do that," Ralph cajoled. "Nothing about this is your fault. You found him though?"

"I did. He was on my porch. I mean, I don't think that's where he was attacked. I think he was left for dead and he was able to make it back to my porch. If the attack happened on my porch, I think I would have heard it. Maybe I could have stopped it."

"Don't do that," Ralph said again. "Maybe you could have interrupted it and now you would both be dead. If Joey made the effort to come back to your porch, it's because he knew you would help him...and you did. That's what you need to remember."

Ralph was trying to focus on comforting Annie, but even as much as he would like for this particular woman to lean on him for emotional and physical support, his mind was already racing to the investigation.

If Joey was attacked in or near Annie Laurie's front yard, then that's where the evidence would be. Fresh evidence. Not already a day old like at Carmilla's. This time there hadn't *been* time for a dozen cars and people to track through the scene. Ralph would need to get back there by daylight, if possible, but he didn't want to leave Annie. Not yet.

"What are the doctors saying about Joey. Will he recover?" Ralph thought bringing Annie's thoughts back to the present moment might help her move out of the regret of the past hours.

"Come with me," she said. "I'll show you."

As they walked back down the hall together, Annie tried to fill Ralph in on Joey's condition. "They're making sure he stays asleep," she said, "because of the pain. Like a medically induced coma, you know? He doesn't really need surgery, not like we think about surgery, but they did give him over a thousand stitches. Four different doctors were stitching him up at the same time. I tried to stay with him, but sometimes when they were cleaning the wounds, I just couldn't watch. It was too awful."

They had reached the room, and Annie took Ralph by the hand to lead him to the bed. Ralph made a momentary note of the way her hand felt in his and filed it away to think about later. There was plenty to think about now.

Joey Morouse was bandaged almost head to toe like a mummy, except that most of his face was showing. Unlike Carmilla, his facial features were not cut to bloody meat confetti. There were obvious scratches on each cheek, and a long set of stitches across his chin, but his eyes, nose and mouth were undamaged.

As if knowing what he must be thinking, Annie Laurie explained. "They say the reason his fore-arms are so badly damaged is because he was defending his face. Also, the doctor says that scrape on his left cheek is just my driveway, like maybe he fell on his face and that's why the killer couldn't cut him there anymore. But the cuts on his arms, on his wrists, are so bad that he would have bled out within five minutes if I hadn't found him and called for an ambulance."

"So, at this point, are they saying he will survive?"

Annie shrugged, and the tears welled up again. "They say if he makes it through tonight, his chances are a lot better."

"Well," Ralph said, trying to smile, "It's already almost morning. Who is the attending doctor?"

Ralph asked this last question of the nurse who had just stepped in to check Joey's vitals. She recognized the question was for her.

"It's Dr. Savory," she said. "Would you like to speak with him?"

"I would," Ralph answered. "Thank you."

The nurse left the room, and while they waited for the doctor to come, Ralph thought again of the undisturbed crime scene on Annie's lawn.

"Annie," he said, "I'm going to need to go back to your place and examine the scene of the attack."

She looked up at him. "Ok…"

"I assume you're going to want to stay here with Joey, but I need to ask for your address, and also can I have a key to get inside? I won't disturb anything in your house, I just need to be able to have a full view of the area…where you were, where he was…?"

Annie was already fishing in her purse for the key. "My address is 3702 Richmond Street. It's in the…"

Ralph interrupted her: "The Village apartments? You live there?"

The incredulity in Ralph's voice gave Annie a confused pause. "Yes…I rented a place when I first moved to Cotton Gorge. I meant to get a real house by now, like a big girl, but I'm comfortable. It's all I need."

She handed Ralph the key and he pocketed it. "No…I mean, that's fine. I'm just surprised because I live there too. I'm at 3706. That means we're almost next-door neighbors…just separated by old Mrs. Perkins."

"Ah, Mrs. Perkins," Annie mused.

"How have I never seen you?"

"I imagine we keep very different hours. You work days and I work nights…mostly." Annie was quiet for a moment. "I don't really have much of a social life. I'm friendly with all the customers at the Possum Hole, but after hours I mostly keep to myself." She looked back down at the deathly still young man on the bed between them. "Joey is kind of my family."

Dr. Savory came in just then, speaking at a volume that sounded like it must surely be nine AM on the happiest of sunny days.

"Hello, Detective!" he boomed, crossing to Ralph and sticking out his hand. "You've come to see our patient, no doubt!"

Ralph winced at the loud voice in the small, quiet room, and shook the doctor's hand. "What do you think, Doc?"

"I think he's had a harder night than either of us!"

Ralph nodded somberly at this obvious assessment.

Dr. Savory moved to the side of the bed and adjusted the tube leading down to the IV port in Joey's hand.

"I think he's going to make it. I think he's going to have a really hard time of it in recovery, but it looks like he's got friends to help see him through it. I think it'll be quite a while before he throws a baseball, if he ever did that sort of thing."

"Not to be indelicate," Ralph began tentatively, "but when you were cleaning him up, stitching him up, did you find anything that might be any kind of clue to who did this?"

The doctor shook his head. "Not really. Not that might be helpful. We did find hay in a couple of the wounds."

"Hay?" Annie and Ralph said almost simultaneously.

"Yes, but that's probably not helpful. Around here, hay is as common as gingivitis. It's my understanding he was attacked outside, on the ground, so it isn't really news that there was some hay and dirt in the wounds. You're thinking this was done by one person?"

"You don't?" Ralph answered the question with a question.

"I don't," Dr. Savory agreed. "A strong young fellow like this, in the whole big out-of-doors? What one person could take him down and cut him this many times without him being able to get away or effectively fight back? The way he's cut up, it would have had to be a gang of several people surrounding him."

Ralph nodded. This was exactly what Mike had been saying about Carmilla. But still…

Ralph stood up straight and nodded his thanks at Dr. Savory. To Annie, he said, "I'm going to go back to your apartment before the scene gets compromised. You try to catch some shut-eye either in here or in the lobby."

"I'll try," she said wearily.

Turning to go, Ralph spoke to her once more. "I'll be back, Annie Laurie Cherry. I'll be back soon, and this is all going to be OK."

Looking relieved, as though she honestly believed that everything would be OK just because Detective Ralph James said so, Annie gave him a thin smile.

Chapter Nine

Joey Morouse had spent half of his childhood cleaning windows and the other half attending Girl Scout meetings with his sisters. The only boy in a family of five children, Joey was caught in that weird other-world of having to conform to all of the activities surrounding the girls, and also recognize that, as the Son-and-Heir, he was expected to grow into taking over the family business: J&R Window Cleaning.

J&R stood for the first names of Joey's parents: Joe and Rachel. The window cleaning part was because Joe, Joey's dad, had promised Rachel that he would build a family business that all their sons could be part of, a real legacy…except Joe and Rachel had girl after girl after girl…and then Joey…and then another girl.

Being an old-fashioned fellow, Joe didn't like to think of his girls having to work, certainly not in Professional Window Cleaning. Even when the older girls wheedled and whined to be taken along to help with the work, Joe said no. A woman's place was in the home, and a man's place was out in the wide world, earning a living.

This point was accentuated in the video that Joe made to advertise his business. Ever the entrepreneur, Joe didn't just hire someone to make a video for him; instead he spent a large chunk of family savings to buy himself a video camera, two monitors, a professional editing board and a microphone. He set all of these up in the little room off the garage which he dubbed "Dad's Office" and went about the lengthy process of learning how to create a J&R Window Cleaning video for himself.

Joe also undertook the job of creating a "brochure" about J&R Window Cleaning, a single copy of a booklet with black and white photos of himself in full uniform and hard hat, cleaning the windows of local businesses. Joe's uniform was really quite admirable; he could afford to make it nice since he was the only person on his staff. In Joe's closet were three identical pair of navy-blue work pants, and three light blue short-sleeved uniform shirts, each with the name Joe stitched over the pocket, and the J&R logo in a patch on the back. Very, very professional.

Joe was quite determined about his video. He carried that camera around with him for weeks, recording bits of sunrise over Hogan House, or just holding it out the window when he was driving, to capture footage of local farms and a scan of downtown. Rachel held the camera a few times to film Joe cleaning windows on businesses and also on various residential homes, expertly maneuvering his squeegee in a pattern that was almost a ballet across the glass.

When Joe got through editing these bits together, he then decided to record Rachel slowly turning through the pages of the brochure while he narrated into the microphone.

In the end, the video was five and a half minutes long, and more than three minutes were the thumbing through of the brochure. Joe's oldest daughter Monica said that she had never heard of someone making a video to advertise a brochure...but Joe was undeterred.

J&R Window Cleaning was the only window cleaning company in Cotton Gorge, and so business was good. Joe kept his prices low and his uniform crisp, and he never failed to show his video to everyone who would sit still for five minutes. It is doubtful the video garnered him any more business than he already had, but it was a point of pride.

Joey was in middle school the year of the video. At thirteen, he hadn't yet earned his J&R professional uniform, but he often went with his Dad in the wee hours before school and worked again until dusk after school, and almost always on weekends. "Someday you'll be the man of the family!" Joe would tell his only son. "And all this will be yours!"

Thirteen-year-old Joey was already remarkably adept at swinging a squeegee. He could even mix his father's perfect cleaning fluid with just the right amount of secret ingredient (lemon juice) to perfection. He enjoyed the work and he enjoyed the people, and he enjoyed the satisfaction of a job well done.

But the idea of "all this" being his didn't interest him at all.

What did interest Joey was the video editing equipment his father had purchased which, after the creation of The Video, was just sort of gathering dust in Dad's Office. Joey would go to the office when he had a little free time and create movies of his sisters making pretend commercials or singing songs they'd learned in glee club. Then after he'd made the recording, he would work with it on the editing board, doing silly things like speeding up his sisters' singing until they sounded like chipmunks (which Joey figured was a vast improvement), or making people disappear from the scene and then reappear unexpectedly. He liked editing in sound effects or clips from actual TV shows or commercials.

When Joey's sisters got tired of performing for him, he turned his burgeoning skills onto Hollywood. By 1983, the local Skaggs grocery store had a small section dedicated to the rental of video tapes. Joey could go on a Saturday night and rent a brand-new blockbuster for about three dollars. The catch was that the new releases had to be returned the very next morning, but one night was plenty of time for Joey to take the movie home, put it in the editing machine, and just record a copy for the family's personal library. The first film he copied in this way was the musical *Annie*, which made his mother and his younger sister very happy.

But when his younger sister was indulging herself in watching *Annie* over and over and over, Rachel began lamenting the one moment in the film when Daddy Warbucks is frustrated and says the word "Damn."

Joey nodded thoughtfully at his mother's concern, and when his sister finished watching the pirated film for the ninth time, he took the cassette back to Dad's Office and worked to correct the problem. Just like he had been able to make one or the other sister disappear from a chipmunk-sounding video in his early days, he could make Daddy Warbucks' extraneous profanity disappear as well. And so he did.

This talent became his life's work. Within just a few months, the Morouse family had an enormous library of films, both old and new, and Joey had worked his special kind of magic to edit out the unacceptable bits like the profanity in *Christine*, and Mandy Patinkin's butt in *Yentl*.

Not only did this skill come in handy for the family, word began to spread such that Joey's editing services were sought by school groups and churches who wanted to show a movie that had one or more less-than-appropriate scenes or phrases. Joe Sr. began insisting that Joey charge for his services, and so he began collecting ten dollars for each edited video, three dollars of which was to cover the rental of the video that was to be corrected.

By the time Joey began charging for the work he was doing, which was in essence both theft and copyright infringement, Joey was sixteen years old. He was still washing windows, though by sixteen, he had his own J&R uniform. A junior in high school, Joey was beginning to consider his college options, and what kind of school might accept him into a program where he could further study film editing, in (hopefully) a setting that would allow him to explore slightly less illegal avenues for creative outlet.

This consideration came to an end when Joe Sr. opened a letter addressed to Joey from Northwestern State University, a letter which stated that the faculty at NSU were thrilled he was considering their AV program, and they would love to meet with Joey and his parents to further discuss Joey's exciting future with NSU.

By the time Joey got home from school that day, his father had gone through several cycles of raging, self-pity, and crying, then back to raging again. Joey walked in on the eleventh period of raging. Joe Sr. met him at the front door, waving the now sadly crumpled NSU letter and insisting that this traitor to his family name was never going to get one penny of support for this foolish college goose-chase.

Joey was caught off guard, but still tried to explain himself, saying that this was his artistic passion, and he needed to pursue it. Rachel, who had unfortunately had to listen to all eleven of Joe Sr.'s emotional cycles, tried to back up her only son…but this seemed to make it worse.

Joe Sr., cycling back into self-pity mode, wound a long yarn of his own upbringing in poverty and how he had been determined to make something better for himself and to set that example for his son, his only son, who was now stabbing him in the back by rejecting the family business that he, Joe Sr., had devoted his life to creating. What is a man without a legacy? Now there would be no legacy. The business would die with him and no one would even remember that Joe Morouse had lived and breathed and worked and given it all for his ungrateful son.

Having exhausted himself in this all-day tirade, Joe. Sr. took himself to bed at five-thirty, and when he awoke the next morning, he went about his business as though none of this had happened. It was never discussed again. But when Joey graduated high school, he and his friend Rodney pooled their funds and rented a tiny A-frame house, and Joey began his long-term plan of saving money for college. He wandered into the Possum Hole before it was open for business, told Annie Laurie Cherry straight up that he had no experience but needed a job. His honesty—and probably just a little bit because of his pretty face—made her hire him to be a bartender. It didn't matter that he'd never done it before; Annie remedied that problem within the two weeks before the Possum Hole opened for customers, and no one ever asked how a kid, barely eighteen years old, managed to be hired as a bartender. The following year, when Louisiana raised the legal drinking age from 18 to 21, Joey was already well-established and his right to serve drinks at 19 was never in question.

The unspoken rift between Joey and his father didn't last very long. By the time the Possum Hole was successfully opened, Joey was already donning his J&R uniform and helping his Dad on Sundays and days off. The only difference was that this time, his father paid him for his work so that Joey could manage his rent and groceries now that he was out on his own.

In the meantime, finally acknowledging the changing world, Joe. Sr. had bought a uniform for his youngest daughter Kathy so that she could learn the family business. Kathy was much more enthusiastic about being heir to the company than Joey was ever going to be.

While Joey lay unconscious in the hospital, he could feel no pain, and he could not assess the passage of time, but *could* absolutely remember what happened, and he could hear the various people who stood over his bed to talk about it. It was so frustrating to have the answers they wanted, to a point, and to not be able to share them! He was aware of his parents when they came to see him, could hear his mother crying and his father blustering about "the bastards who did this to my Joey!" His sisters all visited. He could hear them arguing amongst themselves over which one would brush his hair or shave him, and like everyone else, they bantered their guesses of who had done this terrible thing to *little Joey*.

He could hear Annie, and he ached to tell her he was OK. She felt so bad. She blamed herself. Sometimes when they were alone, she would go on and on, and cry, about how she wished she could do it differently, go back and stop this gang of maniacs. He wanted desperately to tell her that she couldn't have stopped it…but that would have to wait.

Joey could hear the doctor when he came in. Dr. Savory would speak encouragingly to Annie, or to Joey's parents or sisters, but when he was in there just with a nurse, Dr. Savory would speak more frankly, talking about the wounds that were healing and the ones that weren't, changing Joey's meds and checking his vitals all over again, as though the nurses who checked him every hour on the hour might have gotten it wrong. Joey knew they were keeping him asleep. They didn't want him to wake up with all the pain. But Joey needed them to let him wake up! He needed to tell them what he knew!

And then he heard Detective James. He came to "check on our patient" but Joey knew better. He figured Ralph was working the case, but mostly he came to the hospital as an excuse to see Annie.

Or at least Joey hoped so. Annie deserved someone really great in her life. Joey could hear the change in Annie's voice when Ralph came for a visit. Ralph probably couldn't detect it, because he hadn't known Annie as long as Joey had, and that difference in Annie's voice had started almost from day one. Annie never wavered in her concern over Joey, but he could tell she liked it when Ralph came. That was good. Very good. Time for Annie to have a love life of her own instead of always worrying over his.

Sometimes, Joey's love life came to visit him as well. Three girls he had dated briefly showed up that Thursday to stand over the bed and sob and tell Annie, or the doctor, or the nurse, how much he meant to them, how they always knew he was the one, how tragic it had been when they broke up. Joey wanted to laugh out loud. He wanted to remind each one of them exactly why the relationship hadn't worked out. "Liz, you drove me crazy with your list of demands and no, I wasn't ever going to buy you a car. Casey, you literally told me that if I went to my sister's birthday instead of taking you to dinner, we were finished…so we were. Ashley, I'm sorry but I could not waste another hour of my life listening to you talk about the spiritual benefits of yoga."

Once, when Joey was about twelve and he and his Dad were spending a Saturday cleaning windows, Joey fell out of their work van onto the highway.

This was before the seat belt law was enforced, and Joe Sr. had simply never required it. Seat belts were a nuisance in any vehicle and were always tucked way down into the seat, so they didn't get in the way. So, on that day, driving down the highway, listening to Andy Gibb repeatedly insist that he wanted to be Joey's everything, Neither Joey nor his Dad were buckled up. At that time, Joe Sr. was driving a 1972 Ford Econoline Southwestern Bell Telephone van, which he had bought cheap and repainted in the J&R blue and added a giant logo sticker. The van only had the two bucket seats in the front, and the back was empty in order to haul window cleaning equipment.

The whole thing smelled like lemon juice.

The thing is, that telephone van was the Morouse family's only transportation, and so when Joe needed to chauffeur his wife and daughters as well, he threw a twin-sized mattress in the back and all five kids would make themselves comfortable on the mattress while Rachel rode shotgun. In that scenario, nobody had a seat belt.

But on the day in question, Joey was in the passenger seat, leaning with his right arm against the door, singing along with Andy at the top of his twelve-year-old lungs, when the old van hit a bump and Joey's door flew open. Joey didn't even have time to react with a yelp or anything that would alert his father. He rolled noiselessly out of the van and continued to roll over and over until he came to a stop on the shoulder of the road.

Joe Sr., accustomed to the creaking sounds of his work van, did not even notice that the door had come open. Eyes on the road, he only wondered why Joey had stopped singing…and then he turned to look at his son, but only saw the wide-open door, swinging gaily like the tail of a fish enjoying warm water on a sunny day.

Unspeakably mortified, Joe slammed on his brakes and pulled over. Jumping out of the van, he ran like a mad man to the small crowd of people who had gathered on the shoulder about a hundred yards behind where he had stopped. When he arrived, panting and terrified, Joey was just getting to his feet. Relieved that his son was alive and ambulatory, Joe took quick assessment of Joey's cuts and scrapes, knowing that there would be hell to pay when Rachel found out.

Two things happened on that day. First, from then on, anyone sitting in either one of the bucket seats of the J&R Window Cleaning van was wearing a seat belt (there wasn't much to be done for the kids on the mattress in the back) and second, Joey Morouse was deeply committed to the avoidance of pain.

In the seven years since that accident, Joey had been not only invested in keeping himself out of harm's way, but also those that he cared about. For this reason, despite the fact that he knew he was overreacting, he just couldn't let himself ignore it when it looked like Annie was in danger. He had to do whatever it took to protect her. He had to keep her from pain.

Only now, she was definitely in pain, standing over him at all hours, crying sometimes, berating herself at other times. The cocktail of meds in Joey's IV was keeping him from any pain, but Annie was getting the brunt of it.

No matter how much he knew it was going to hurt, Joey was ready to wake up so that he could tell Annie and Ralph, and anyone else who needed to know, what happened to him, and who did this. Maybe he didn't have all the answers, but he definitely had more than anyone else was able to offer right now.

If only he could open his eyes.

Chapter Ten

As both a beat cop and a detective, Ralph had been required to go into all kinds of houses and apartments and vehicles and landfills in order to investigate or interview or gather evidence. He once went into a house in Shreveport that was wall-to-wall dog shit, and the only thing sitting out in the middle of the living room was a gallon of milk. No refrigerator, no furniture, but there sat an almost full gallon of milk.

Though Ralph had an acute ability for quickly seeking out and finding what he was looking for in any setting, he had also grown accustomed to pretty much ignoring everything about a residence except for whatever it was he was looking for. In his last year as a beat cop, he took a call to see a woman whose home had been broken into. She had lost a camera, a coin collection which had been framed and hanging on the wall, (that's pretty much thug code for "Ooh! Ooh! Steal ME!") and a small box of costume jewelry which was probably worth about twenty dollars. The fun part was that in his hurry to stuff her belongings into his backpack, the thief had not maintained control of his own, such that right in the middle of the floor of her hallway she had found a carelessly rolled up set of release papers, showing that this fellow, Pete Arnold, had only been out of the Caddo Parish jail for about ten days before going back to his life of petty crime.

Name, inmate number, release date, probation officer…all of this information was on those papers, and Ralph was able to immediately track him down. But looking back on the whole incident, he realized that he had no functional memory of the woman's house. He had gone in for what he needed, and came out with nothing extra.

In the process of taking that woman's statement, Ralph had to ask her if she had ever invited Pete Arnold into her house. "No!" she insisted. "And after this behavior, he can forget it!"

In all the years of traipsing through people's houses or digging through their belongings, Ralph had never genuinely felt like he was *snooping*...until he was snooping through Annie Laurie Cherry's apartment.

He had run in sort of a zig zag pattern around Cotton Gorge that morning. He went to Annie's apartment first, in the very early dawn, but he didn't go inside. Initially, he just studied the actual crime scene, noting that the attack must have taken place on the sidewalk, as the blood spatter there was overt and obvious. The path Joey had taken to get himself back to Annie's porch wasn't as obvious, though Ralph could assume Joey dragged himself across the most direct trajectory through the grass. In her haste to follow the ambulance, Annie had driven her own car through the grass in order to get around Joey's truck which was parked behind hers in the driveway. That necessary maneuver had obliterated any sign there might have been of Joey's trip from the sidewalk to the porch. The little concrete slab that was the porch, of course, was almost completely covered in blood stain.

Ralph studied the spot on the sidewalk where the attack must have happened. It had to have been a blitz attack for Joey to have made so little noise that Annie never heard him. Maybe Joey was in the process of unlocking his truck when he was attacked from behind. That would make the most sense. A healthy young man who was already on high guard would have had to be attacked from behind in order to be taken down like he was. That could also mean that he never saw his attacker, such that even when he awoke, he might not have any helpful information.

Rather than go directly inside Annie's apartment once he had studied the yard, Ralph instead went back to Carmilla's house. After the discussions with Mike and with Dr. Savory, he wanted to give that scene another once-over. The front door of Carmilla's little house was taped shut with yellow "crime scene" tape, but Ralph used the key he'd taken from Carmilla's belongings the last time he was here and, unsealing the tape, he opened the door.

The first time he'd come to Carmilla's house, he was with Mike, and they talked the whole time about all the details of the murder and the bloody scene in the garage. This time, on his own, Ralph took the time to go room to room, kind of getting to know Carmilla Rabbi. What was it about this woman that made her a victim of this terrible crime?

The house felt a little like stepping back about twenty years. Like a live-in time capsule. The *Home Interiors* décor, the macramé plant holders, the red glass wall sconces, the mottled shag carpet…this did not feel like the house of a woman in her mid-thirties. He understood that Carmilla had not been wealthy, but this wasn't just about an inability to afford newer things, this felt like a house that had been genuinely loved when it was first taken in hand…but nothing had changed in a very long time.

When he stepped down the hallway and studied the old elementary school pictures of what was surely little Carmilla, he understood. This had been her parents' house, and she hadn't ever made it her own. Somehow, that made this whole story seem even sadder to Ralph. Carmilla Rabbi seemed to have had nothing. No friends, no family, no appreciable personality, and no home that she could call hers. If the murderers had left Carmilla in her garage instead of moving her to Drew Marshall's dumpster, she might have lain there for weeks before anyone noticed. Maybe a lot longer.

So what was it about this sad inconspicuous woman that had caught the attention of the killers? Joey's attack might have been opportunistic—after all, he was out on the sidewalk in the middle of the night—but Carmilla's attack was a home invasion. It appeared the killers had been waiting for her, had chosen her…but why?

Ralph wrapped up his study into Carmilla's despondent life and re-taped the front door.

Still not ready to go to Annie's apartment, Ralph drove instead to the dilapidated little A-frame house that matched the address on Joey Morouse's driver's license. He had the key that was in his bag of personal effects at the hospital, but the car in the driveway meant Joey's roommate, Rodney Kirkland, was home and likely to let him in.

Rodney met him at the door wearing a towel around his waist.

"Sorry, man," he said after Ralph expertly flashed his badge. "I'm just headed to work. You can come in though. If you're still here when I leave, just lock up, would ya?"

Rodney had heard the news about Joey through the gossip vine but didn't seem overly concerned for his friend. He appeared to believe that Joey could handle anything, and that he would visit his buddy in the hospital after work. He then retreated into his bedroom, and Ralph's only subsequent awareness of Rodney was when he heard the front door shut and the car in the driveway fire up and pull out.

Ralph didn't exactly know what he was looking for here. He hoped he would know it when he saw it. If the attack on Carmilla was premeditated, then the attack on Joey probably was as well, and that meant there had to be some sort of connection between the two of them. What was he not seeing?

He had no reason to believe they'd had any relationship. Annie certainly didn't think so. While it sounded like Joey had a long string of ex-girlfriends, they all seemed to fit into the Young & Perky category, a category Carmilla may never have inhabited.

Ralph wandered into Joey's bedroom. The bed was unmade, and the only chair was occupied by an enormous pile of laundry, which may have been clean, or dirty, or both. The surface of the dresser was scattered with hair products and deodorants and spray bottles, a brush, a comb, an unplugged hair dryer, and a mélange of loose change intermingled with all of it.

On the wall over the bed was a large poster displaying the cover of U2's *Joshua Tree* album, and beside the dresser was another poster of the Teenage Mutant Ninja Turtles. On the ceiling was a pin-up of Heather Locklear. A simple bookshelf in the corner revealed that Joey was interested in woodworking, not only because of the books about woodworking, but because it appeared the bookshelf was one of his handicrafts. It was nothing to write home about, but it was solid. There was a stack of random magazines about computers and filmmaking and muscle cars; none of them had an address sticker, so it appeared Joey bought them at will in the grocery check-out.

On the bedside table was a copy of Stephen King's *Misery*, and what appeared to be a little van made out of popsicle sticks. It was painted blue and had a sticker on the side with the letters J&R. On the top, written in magic marker, was the message, "Buckle-up! Love, Monica."

This was most definitely the room of a nineteen-year-old boy.

The little work shed behind the house revealed very little more. Basic yardwork implements, some tools for the previously established woodworking interest, and several boxes of what appeared to be clothes and books, none of which were weathering very well. There were no clues here, just as there were no clues at Carmilla's.

The only clue Ralph had gathered so far was that neither crime scene had any evidence of hay. Not even the smallest piece. This would have to mean that, in some way, the killer or killers were bringing their own…and that made no sense.

By now it was lunchtime, and Ralph imagined that Annie hadn't had anything to eat. He left Joey's house, remembering to lock the front door behind him, and made the drive back to the hospital. He saw Annie's car still parked in the ER parking lot, so he walked with confidence to the ICU and into Joey's room.

Three young women, all with Joey's black curls and green eyes, were fussing over him in the bed while Annie appeared to be half asleep in the room's only chair. She looked up when Ralph came in the room, and he saw her sit up straight in an attempt to appear more alert than she felt. Ralph went to her and placed a hand on her shoulder.

"Any new word?"

"Not yet," she said, standing to face him. "His family has been in and out." Here, she indicated the three young women whom Ralph had already assumed were sisters. "I think they're going to move him out of ICU in a few hours, into a regular room, and maybe let him wake up. Or at least stop forcing him to stay asleep. They can't say how long he might be out on his own."

"You've been here the whole time?"

"Yes."

"Have you eaten at all?"

"Oh…" Annie took a moment to consider. "I guess not."

"Well it looks like Joey is in good hands for a while. Why don't you let me take you for a bite and we'll be back before he knows you're gone."

On the one hand, Ralph hoped this sounded like the sort of offer any officer of the law might make…you know, "to serve and protect." On the other hand, he kind of hoped it sounded like "can I buy you lunch?" and that, hearing it this way, she would say yes.

However she heard it, she didn't say yes. She didn't say anything. She just picked up her purse and headed for the door. Ralph followed.

Assuming she didn't want hospital cafeteria food, Ralph led the way to the front entrance of the hospital and she accompanied him, wordlessly, to his car. Once settled and buckled in the passenger seat, Annie crumpled from exhaustion.

"You should have heard his mother," she said, and Ralph heard the tears threatening her voice as he maneuvered the Sable out onto the highway. "She kept saying how she could hardly recognize her baby. She cried and prayed and she kept asking me questions about how it happened, and I don't have a clue! What could I tell her? And his dad was so angry…the kind of angry that's just grief turned inside out. I just feel like this is all my fault. If it hadn't been for me, he wouldn't have been there."

Now the tears began to fall, and Ralph reached across her to open the glove box where there was a stack of napkins of various sizes from a variety of fast food establishments. Sniffling, Annie reached in and helped herself to two or three of them, then shut the compartment with a slam. While she wiped her tears, Ralph took the opportunity to comfort her with some police work.

"Listen," he said, not making eye contact. "Joey was a target. If he'd been at his own house, he'd have been attacked there. If he'd stayed at work late, he'd have been attacked there. If he'd gone to a midnight movie, chances are he would have been attacked there. The only difference it made that you were close by is that, thanks to you, he's in the hospital instead of the morgue right now."

Annie considered this with a look of puzzlement.

"You think he was a target? Not just a victim of convenience?"

"That's right. The first victim, Carmilla, she was attacked in her home. All evidence points to the killer or killers were already there when she got home from work. Waiting for her. She was chosen. Now, sometimes, when there's a killing spree, the first victims are chosen and then it kind of starts getting random, but that's not so likely between just the first victim and the second."

"So…" Annie chewed on this idea. "If Joey was a chosen target, why was he chosen?"

Ralph ground his jaw for a moment. "That's what I'm trying to figure out. I haven't found anything yet that connects the dots between Joey and Carmilla. They didn't exactly move in the same circles."

"I wouldn't think so, no."

They were pulling into the drive through at Hardee's and Ralph rolled down his window to order two mushroom swiss burgers, two large fries, and two Cokes. "I wish I could tell you I usually try to eat healthier than this, but that wouldn't exactly be true," he admitted with a wince.

Annie smiled warmly. "The impressive napkin assortment was kind of a giveaway," she said.

Ralph eased the car into a spot facing away from the Hardee's and they ate mostly in silence. As she closed the cardboard box her burger had come in, Annie finally spoke. "Thank you for this."

"Desperate times call for desperate measures," Ralph said, crumpling his last three French fries into his mouth.

Back at the hospital, Ralph simply let Annie out at the door. Leaning over to speak to her out the window, he said, "Call me at the station if there's any change!"

"I will!" she promised, and waved as she turned toward the entrance.

Back on the highway, Ralph decided it was time to do the thing he had been putting off: go over Annie's apartment.

He had meant to sound convincing when he told Annie that Joey had been a target and that her presence had not in any way contributed to the attack. He wanted that to be absolutely true…but there was still the lingering possibility that Annie herself had been the target, and that Joey simply got in the way. That would be a very upsetting scenario for Annie, and Ralph hoped it wasn't true, but he couldn't dismiss the possibility just because he didn't want to see Annie cry.

On Richmond Street, Ralph drove past Annie's driveway and parked in his own. The caffeine from his lunch Coke was making him feel slightly more awake than he had earlier, but he knew he needed to get some sleep. He'd be no help to anyone if he didn't. He comforted himself with the thought that he could do a pass through Annie's place and then come back to his own for a powernap. As he got out of his car, Mrs. Perkins came out of her front door to greet him.

"What's this I hear?" she asked him without clarifying what she had heard.

"There was some trouble here last night, Mrs. Perkins," Ralph answered as he walked toward her. "A friend of your neighbor's got hurt out on the sidewalk. He's in the hospital and he's going to be OK. Are you OK?"

Mrs. Perkins was in her seventies, and very frail. She seemed always to be in a nightgown with a loose bathrobe, no matter what the time of day, and most often with brush rollers in her hair. Ralph could only picture her with the brush rollers, so he couldn't have testified to what the rollers made her hair look like. He'd never been inside her apartment, but almost every day he saw her there on her porch, in her nightgown and brush rollers, fussing over a little sapling that she had planted two years previously. It looked like it might be a weeping willow, if it would ever grow up, and Mrs. Perkins doted over it like a child. She watered it and trimmed it and talked to it. Perhaps the trimming was the reason it never seemed any bigger. At present, the little willow only boasted two thin branches forking off of its little trunk, and the few leaves it managed to grow in the summer had already fallen. Even in its current naked state, Mrs. Perkins doted over it. It was the only thing that seemed to get her out of her apartment at all.

"Yes, I'm OK," she said in her wavering voice. "I've been trying to call my friend Effie, but she doesn't answer. Do you know where she is?"

"No, ma'am," Ralph said in the kind of condescending voice that people use for the elderly. He heard it, and he hated it, and that's what came out anyway. "I don't know where she is. But I bet if you keep calling, she'll pick up."

"This thing that keeps happening, like what happened here last night...you don't think that happened to Effie, do you? Should you go to her house? She won't answer her phone."

"I really don't think so," Ralph said. "I'm trying to figure out what happened last night, but I'm sure your friend is fine."

Mrs. Perkins' eyes got watery. "It's a scary world," she said. "I just don't know what to do anymore."

Ralph's heart went out to her. It *was* a scary world, and he had the physical and mental tools to deal with it...mostly. He couldn't imagine being her age, lost in everything that was modern, unsure from day to day whether her own body or mind would hold together for another 24-hour cycle.

"I guess we're all just trying to find our way, Mrs. Perkins. Just trying to find what makes us happy," Ralph smiled at his elderly neighbor as he passed on his way to Annie's blood-stained porch.

That feeling of *snooping* hit him almost as soon as he had closed the door behind himself. Annie's apartment was a perfect mirror image of his in its structural layout, but in every other way, it was distinctly *her*. The living room furniture was a little shabby, but it matched, and it was clean. The kitchen was neat and cheery, and he could tell that she was the sort of person who actually enjoyed cooking. The shelf in the hallway had a long row of Star Wars action figures, lined up in perfect order, all still in their original packaging.

In jagged contrast to the rest of the house, Annie's bedroom looked like a crime scene in itself. The bed was unmade, and clothes were thrown everywhere. He recalled the timeline she had shared with him. She had come home, fixed a bite to eat, put on her night clothes, gotten in bed...and then heard Joey on the porch. When the ambulance came, she hurriedly changed back into street clothes and followed Joey to the hospital.

Besides the obvious aftermath of her frantic response to Joey's condition, the bedroom looked as tidy as the rest of the house. On the dresser, Ralph spotted a wooden double picture frame with the words "Mom and Dad" carved into the wood. Curious, Ralph moved closer to look at the images of Annie's parents, only to find that they were pictures of Mary Tyler Moore, and Mr. Spock.

More interesting to Ralph than the bedroom was the 2nd bedroom, the door to which was closed with a sign hanging on it which said, "DO NOT OPEN UNTIL CHRISTMAS."

Never one for minding rules like that, Ralph opened the door, and then stood in astonishment. The second bedroom of Annie's apartment was a mini winter-wonderland. There were five fully decorated, although different, Christmas trees, hand-cut paper snowflakes hanging from the ceiling, a full Christmas village along one wall, and a train track that ran the whole perimeter of the room. The floor looked like snow drifts, a wall shelf supported at least thirty glass Santa figurines, and in the far corner a full-sized stuffed Rudolph oversaw the whole thing. Ralph could see at least three power strips each filled with plugs and he imagined that when they were turned on, this room must burst to life with lights and sounds.

Someday soon, Ralph would come to understand Annie's story, to understand how a little girl who had been raised to believe that everything about Christmas was evil—that the music and the lights and the colors and the presents were all just the Devil tempting her to sin—would grow into a woman who insisted on having a part of her life that was Christmas all year long. This, however, was not that day, and Ralph found the Christmas Room beyond baffling.

Even so, something else was beginning to insist on drawing his attention. How long had it been since he had tended his addiction? How long, exactly?

Ralph tried to remember. It had been a very long night. It was four in the morning when he got the call about Joey, five by the time he got to the hospital, seven by the time he got to Annie's yard, noon by the time he got to Hardee's…his last fix must have been at about 2 am, so that meant, by now, it had been about twelve hours.

He should never, ever go twelve hours.

Before he started thinking about that timeline, he was being reminded of his need by the unmistakable feeling behind his eyes that made him blink more than usual. Once he started calculating how many hours it had been, the pressure in his head mounted into full-on withdrawals.

Ralph quickly left Annie's house to head back to his car where relief waited, but just as he passed Mrs. Perkins' door, she flung it open. "You think we're just supposed to find a way to be happy?" she said forcefully, accusatorily.

Stunned for a second, Ralph stopped in his tracks and blinked at Mrs. Perkins, then started trying to answer, "I mean…"

But she wasn't interested. Mrs. Perkins turned away, grabbed the two puny branches of her willow tree in both hands, and ripped them down and away from the trunk, then flung them on the ground at Ralph's feet. "Be happy!" she shouted at him, then stormed back into her apartment and slammed the door.

Ralph stood stock still, unsure how to categorize what had just happened. He had so many things he needed to do, but he also knew he couldn't just walk away when his neighbor was obviously having some kind of episode.

Forgetting his original mission, Ralph went instead into his own apartment and called Hogan House.

"Cotton Gorge Police Department, this is Desiree speaking. How may I direct your call?"

"Desi, it's Ralph."

"Oh, Ralph…what a day you're having. Have you eaten?"

Ralph appreciated Desi's motherly concern. "I have, thanks. Listen, you know my next-door neighbor?"

"Myra Perkins?"

"Yes…who would I talk to that's kind of a…next of kin?"

"Oh my…"

'No, no!" Ralph interjected, realizing he'd given Desi the wrong impression. "I just had an encounter with her that was worrying. I think she needs someone to check on her. Someone who knows her and can make decisions if she needs help."

"Ah. OK. Well, her oldest daughter lives in Minden. If you give me a few minutes, I can call you back with her phone number."

While Ralph waited for Desi to call back, he went over what he had learned from his investigatory morning that might be helpful in tracking down the murderous gang…which was basically diddly-over-squat. There wasn't any connection that he could see between Carmilla and Joey or Carmilla and Annie…and he really had just been *snooping* in Annie's apartment.

Once he knew Mrs. Perkins' daughter was on her way, he started to go back to his car…and then remembered. Now another whole hour had passed, and he still hadn't dosed himself. Panic began to set in, because now he knew it was too late. Now the pain was coming, and there was no way to stop it.

He went back into the privacy of his apartment anyway and did the deed. He went to his bed to lie down in hopes that gravity would help the drug take effect, but he knew it was no use. He would have to go all the way down into the suffering now before he could come back up again. As his whole head throbbed with the consequences of his carelessness, Ralph berated himself for being stupid, for being an addict, for letting the drug rule his life.

Everything hurt. God it hurt. He could hardly see, and the light was like a knife piercing his skull. Ralph closed the curtains to try to bring night into his bedroom and lay there moaning in agony waiting for the drug to save him.

At about three-thirty, his phone rang, and he was vaguely aware that Annie was on the other end of the line. Her voice sounded a thousand miles away. She was asking him something, something about Joey, but his head felt like the Hindenburg just before *oh the humanity*, and whatever he said back to her probably didn't make much sense. It didn't even sound like his voice. Then the call was over. She must have said goodbye. Maybe he did too.

At five o'clock, she was standing over his bed.

"How long did you go between doses?" she asked him.

"What?" Ralph raised his head from his pillow and squinted in the light coming from the hallway.

"How long?"

He dropped back to the pillow. "Way too long. About thirteen hours. I shouldn't go more than eight."

"How long ago did you dose?"

"About three."

"Well, I think you should do it again now. I got you a fresh bottle, sometimes that helps."

Without asking any further questions, Ralph sat up and let her help him apply the drug that might get him out of this pit of despair. As she recapped the magic vial, he asked her, "How did you know?"

"The question should be how could I *not* know," she said, sitting on the side of the bed with a smile. "You have like seven bottles of this stuff in your glove box, and when I called you earlier, you sounded like someone had surgically removed your entire sinus system. Those two things together add up to a nasty addiction to over-the-counter nasal spray, if I ever saw one. And I did."

"You did?"

"My Mom," she nodded. "My Mom was addicted for at least a decade. She used to say we could take her bottle of nasal spray from her cold, dead hands."

"It's been thirteen years for me," Ralph admitted. The dose she had given him had begun to break up the tightness in his nasal passages, and the result was snot. Snot flowed from his nose as his eyes began to run with the relief of the pressure. Annie was ready for that part too and handed him a box of tissue she had brought into the bedroom. Ralph sat up to let the juices run as he slowly, sip by sip, began testing his ability to breathe through his ravaged and angry nose.

Any guilt he had felt for stumbling upon Annie's fictional parents and secret winter hideout had been, he believed, equalized by Annie discovering his own darker truth. Now that he was upright and breathing freely for the first time in hours, Annie was able to tell him what she had come for.

Joey Morouse was awake.

Chapter Eleven

Woodson McGuffee had always been a big man. Or, rather, he was a big child who grew into a big man. Woodson's mother had always advocated for "clean your plate so you will grow up big and strong!"

Woodson had merely grown up big.

To hear his father tell it, a man named Joshua McGuffee had sailed on the Mayflower, and when the original settlers landed at Plymouth Rock, Joshua had sneaked off alone in the night to make his way to what would later become Cotton Gorge. By the time Thomas Jefferson swindled the Louisiana territory away from the French, the McGuffee farm was well established as the most profitable enterprise north of New Orleans.

Woodson grew up accepting this story as whole-heartedly as he accepted his grandmother's insistence that jelly is made from banana bruises. This is why he ate neither jelly nor bananas. The McGuffee farm was an indelible part of his place in the world, and Woodson was never going to let it go.

Unfortunately, this plan was made difficult by the fact that Woodson had no children, and no siblings who might have children. Woodson was the last of the McGuffee line. He had considered getting married when he was younger. He had dated Gloria Kickle for several months when he was just out of high school, but the tragic prom incident really brought that to an end.

Woodson and his friend Owen were going to double date for prom that year, with Gloria and Gloria's friend Judy MacAlpine. Owen and Judy were just friends, but Woodson intended to make prom the event that moved his relationship with Gloria from *semi-*

dating to *committed relationship.* To that end, Woodson had saved his money and bought a pretty little promise ring with Gloria's birthstone. He had the idea of slipping it on her finger during a slow dance. He daydreamed about this for weeks, and in his fantasy, the song playing for the slow dance was *Can't Take My Eyes Off You* and Woodson was crooning along softly in Gloria's ear.

In the daydream, Woodson could sing.

Owen was buying flowers for Judy, so Woodson knew he needed to present something at the beginning of the evening so that Gloria didn't feel neglected. He knew Gloria had a sweet tooth, so he bought a "Dairy Box" of assorted chocolates and put a red bow on top. He just knew this was going to be the perfect evening…the one that secured the rest of his life.

What Woodson didn't know is that Owen, feeling a bit insecure about his flower choice, actually showed it to Judy the day before the dance. Trying not to utterly spoil the surprise, he told Judy that Woodson had bought these flowers for Gloria. Judy gushingly told Owen that the flowers were beautiful, and that Gloria would love them, and that of course she would keep the secret.

But of course, she didn't.

Owen went away feeling much more confident about his taste in colorful vegetation, and Judy went straight to Gloria to tell her about the beautiful flowers Woodson had bought for her.

Unsuspecting of any trouble to come, Woodson showed up at Gloria's door on prom night with a box of chocolates in his hand and a promise ring snugly in the pocket of his suit jacket. When Gloria opened the door for him, resplendent in her sky-blue prom dress, Woodson proffered the chocolates, and Gloria's smile faded into a look of puzzlement.

"Candy?" she asked.

"Sweets for my sweet!" Woodson said, having practiced that line several times in his truck on the way over.

"But...where are my flowers?"

"Oh," Woodson's face fell. "I didn't buy flowers. I thought you would like to have the chocolates."

"But you did buy flowers...Judy saw them!"

Woodson had no response to this. He just looked at Gloria.

"Owen showed Judy the flowers you bought!" Gloria was shouting now, and her parents came into view in the doorway behind her.

Utterly confused, Woodson stumbled through any attempt to make sense of what was happening. "Owen bought flowers for Judy, but I thought you might like chocolates."

"So, I'm not good enough for flowers after all?" Gloria railed at him. "I'm just the fat girl who gets candy for prom??"

Woodson's face burned. What was happening to his perfect evening? "Gloria, I don't..."

However Woodson might have finished that sentence was lost to history, as in that moment, Gloria snatched the Dairy Box from his hands and threw it over his shoulder out into the yard. The box opened and an expensive assortment of milk chocolates scattered across the grass. The red bow detached and landed against a pinecone, which was abruptly of equal value to the ruined Dairy Box.

Gloria was now sobbing, and her parents led her away from the door and into the bowels of the house. Standing there gaping, with his heart pounding so hard that he could feel the ring box jolt in his pocket with every beat, Woodson stood there on the porch for a minute before finally reaching in to quietly close the front door.

Six weeks later, right after graduation, Judy and Owen got married. Gloria and Woodson were both in the wedding party, but they didn't speak to each other at all. In the mid-seventies, Owen finally told Woodson that Gloria had said the reason she didn't want to go to prom with Woodson was because even if she sat all the way next to the passenger side door of his truck, she was still squished up against Woodson because he was so big.

This was helpful. Woodson would rather think that his one shot at finding a wife was derailed because she was just mean and petty than because he made the horrible mistake of choosing candy over flowers.

Woodson put the promise ring away in his bottom dresser drawer and turned his attention to the farm.

As a young man, Woodson was able to help out with the basic chores and labor of farm life, but as his father got older and needed more help, so did Woodson's knees. Together, the men decided it was time for them to officially become supervisors and to hire out all the labor that was needed for a working farm.

The trouble was that a working farm didn't actually make enough money to support the McGuffee family and also pay for a full staff of laborers. It was at this point that Woodson really found his creative calling.

The idea began in the fall of 1976. Woodson's father was almost entirely an indoor-farmer by that time, and the full brunt of farm responsibility had fallen to Woodson. One day, when Woodson was looking over their crop of pumpkins, calculating how much the orange gourds would sell for on market day, or if they could even sell them all, his imagination took over.

As Woodson stood there, counting pumpkins as he had every autumn as far back as he could recall, he saw a particularly large pumpkin and had the thought, "That one could be turned into Cinderella's coach!" Then, instead of laughing off this flight of fancy, Woodson allowed his mind to wander further. What if this whole pumpkin patch was enchanted? What would people pay for an enchanted pumpkin?

Within two weeks, Woodson had taken out an ad in several local papers and painted a huge colorful road sign that proclaimed "McGuffee Magical Pumpkin Patch!" Immediately, parents began paying $3 each to bring their children; Woodson's mother would gather the children and read them an original story about a magic pumpkin, and then Woodson would lead them to the Magical Pumpkin Patch where each child would choose a pumpkin to take home. A pumpkin that might have sold at market for seventy-five cents had now become a three-dollar pumpkin.

That first year, between the individual visitors and the school groups, the McGuffee Magical Pumpkin Patch took in enough revenue to pay the laborers until summer.

Riding the high of success, Woodson began expanding. The next autumn, he added features like a corn field maze (which attracted the older kids), and he invested in a Polaroid Instant Camera so that he could charge an extra dollar to take photos of the kids with their personal enchanted pumpkins. That year, the pumpkin patch was so popular that they ran out of pumpkins, and Woodson had to drive to the farmer's market in Mooringsport to restock. He brought the truckload of purchased pumpkins home and placed them haphazardly around the empty pumpkin patch, and not one single child or parent seemed to notice the ruse.

Over the next decade, the McGuffee Magical Pumpkin Patch added something new every year, and every year that October-through-November venture was the farm's salvation. Still a working farm, Woodson oversaw the other crops through the rest of the year, but it was the annual Pumpkin Patch that kept it all going.

In 1982, Woodson's expansion idea included ordering ink pens that bore the name and phone number of the Magical Pumpkin Patch. This hadn't been his idea at first, but he received a phone call from a marketing company in Monroe, offering personalized engraved "high quality" ink pens, and Woodson had a vision of the future. He saw himself passing out so many of the pens that he would wind up having them handed back to him at stores and banks and dry-cleaning establishments. Everyone from the Texas state line to the muddy shores of the Mississippi would hear of the McGuffee Magical Pumpkin Patch, and the visitor count would triple!

Eagerly, Woodson worked with the marketing company to expedite the order. The representative he worked with called him several times to get further details, to offer different kinds of pens and different kinds of fonts, to be sure he had the correct spelling of McGuffee. Woodson had several near-sleepless nights awaiting the delivery of the two hundred pens.

When the box arrived, Woodson tore into it and then stood over his marketing treasure in the kind of dismay previously reserved for watching his suddenly-ex-girlfriend throw a box of chocolates onto her front lawn.

Inside the plain brown box, which was adorned only with Woodson's handwritten name and address, was a loose pile of two hundred cheap plastic pens, all adorned in blue and white stripes—nothing like the shiny black lidded pens Woodson had ordered—and printed on each one was the phrase "A SPECIAL PEN FOR A SPECIAL FRIEND."

Not the family name, nothing about the farm, nothing even close to what Woodson had ordered.

Certain this could be fixed, Woodson immediately went to the telephone and called the number of the company in Monroe, but he was greeted with the ominous three tones, followed by the message, "the number you have dialed has been disconnected or is no longer in service; if you feel you have reached this recording in error, please hang up and try your call again."

Hanging up and trying again only earned him the same recorded message. Woodson realized he'd been had. He'd spent sixty dollars on those pens.

Determined not to be a loser, Woodson came up with a new plan. He painted the roadside sign that year in blue and white stripes and advertised "Bring a Special Friend to the McGuffee Magical Pumpkin Patch!" …and then he offered the pens for sale at fifty cents each. He sold out in the first three weekends of October and was sorry he couldn't order more.

By 1987, forty-year-old Woodson McGuffee was almost entirely immobile. Between the weight of his bulk and the arthritis in his knees, he could hardly get out of bed, let alone go out to the field…but he did it. He sat there in his rocking chair and supervised the laborers and fretted about the kids who—thinking of the Magical Pumpkin Patch as a year-round playground—played tag in his corn even when it wasn't a maze.

On that particular Friday morning in October, Woodson was looking forward to the opening weekend of the Pumpkin Patch, and his workers were getting everything set up. Woodson sat in front of his corn field, rocking and enjoying the autumn breeze, when he heard the commotion. He could hear his workers moving quickly through the corn about twenty yards from where he sat, and then they were talking rapidly, their exclamations overlapping such that he couldn't understand any of it.

Laboriously, he rose from his chair and pushed his girth between the corn stalks, making his way to the epicenter of the upset. He found his workers gathered around what, at first, Woodson mistook for a wild hog that had been killed. This had happened before.

But on closer inspection, he realized that this bloody carcass was too big to be even a really large hog, and also not nearly hairy enough. Woodson leaned over in an attempt to understand what he was looking at…and then he realized. This disfigured hulk, mangled and bloodied beyond perception, was human. Or at least it had been.

Rising in revulsion, Woodson's first thought was that this was not the best marketing strategy for the Magical Pumpkin Patch.

Chapter Twelve

Once the recovery process began, Ralph was restored to normal within about twenty minutes. Miraculous. This is why he'd never been able to get off the stuff, because of the miraculous.

The addiction had begun innocently enough: Ralph was twenty, working full time at Brock's Collision Center in Bossier, and taking night classes at LSU-Shreveport. Between work and school, Ralph had no time to be sick, and so when he woke up one day in August with a stuffy head, he went to Eckerd's for anything that might help—including a little bottle of "instant relief" 12-hour nasal spray.

He made it through that day without ever opening the bottle, but late that night, as Ralph finally tucked his weary body in bed, his stuffy nose predicted he wouldn't be getting any sleep at all.

At first, he wasn't sure he had done it right. The muscle memory that controlled the "squeeze and snort" action in subsequent years didn't exactly come naturally, and Ralph struggled a bit before giving up. Convinced he hadn't done it correctly, he climbed back in bed, certain he was simply destined to mouth-breathe his way through a difficult night.

But then it happened. The miraculous.

After about four minutes, Ralph's nasal passages opened up to a breadth he'd never experienced. Air flowed into his body like a symphony. He could almost hear the choir of angels heralding this otherworldly celebration of proboscal respiration. The air itself was cooler, more refined than Ralph had ever known. He slept like a baby that night and awoke bright eyed and clear-breathing.

But the bottle wasn't kidding when it said 12-hours. At about noon, Ralph's choir of angels sounded more like a pygmy marmoset banging on pots and pans. He hadn't brought the bottle with him, so he ducked into Skaggs on his lunch break and bought another one, not realizing this was the beginning of a long, slippery slope. The second bottle was a different brand, but it had the same effect. Miraculous. Choir of angels.

At bedtime, the stuffiness was coming on again, and so Ralph warded it off proactively, realizing he was getting the hang of the *squeeze-and-snort*.

For the rest of that week, he carried a bottle with him in the car and kept the other by his bed at home. Every twelve hours, he did a shot, and it was like he'd never learned to breathe before this. He passed all the other poor schmucks in his life, the sad sacks who were breathing on their own, utterly oblivious to the bliss that could be theirs for about two dollars a bottle.

On Friday night, He used the last of the bottle by his bed and tossed it in the trash. On Saturday afternoon, he used the last of the bottle in his car and tossed it in the trash. On Saturday night, he remembered he hadn't gotten more, and he thought, "Oh well…I'm not feeling sick anymore. It's not like I need it."

But the Gods of Human Functionality had other plans. By two AM, Ralph's nasal passages were swollen shut to a degree that it felt like a tiny Thor was gripping them tightly shut and *S-Q-U-E-E-Z-I-N-G* with all his might until tears were wrung from Ralph's eyes. Stumbling to the bathroom, Ralph dug in the trashcan for the little empty bottle. With tear-stained vision, he read the fine print on the back label: "WARNING-do not use for more than three days. If condition persists, see your physician."

It had been six days, and Ralph was utterly physically dependent on the nasal spray.

In a sad daze, he spent the next ninety miserable minutes driving around Shreveport looking for an open convenience store that sold the illicit nectar that would get him through the night.

Over the course of the next decade, Ralph's chemical dependence followed the predictable course of any addiction. He had started out with the name brand products, and then dropped to slightly less expensive, and finally resorted to the absolute generic. A dose of one snort per nostril every twelve hours gradually became two snorts every six hours, eight at most. Sometimes it took three snorts. Sometimes it only lasted two hours.

Even though he had bottles stashed all over the place, he would often discover, while traveling, that he had failed to pack one, or failed to bring the one he packed with him from his car or from his hotel, etc., and then a large part of his trip was taken up with finding his next fix before the need found him.

He became a connoisseur of the different types of nasal spray. There were generally two different base drugs, only one of which was in each bottle; Ralph's drug of choice was oxymetazoline hydrochloride, and on pain of death, he must never confuse it with phenylephrine hydrochloride. He made that mistake a couple of times in the early years and deeply regretted it. When his nose was jonesing for its poison, it was a very specific poison…and poisoning it with the wrong drug resulted in Ralph becoming terribly ill for the six-to-twelve hours that the wrong poison ruled his life.

Twice, in the first decade of his addiction, Ralph had tried speaking with a doctor about the problem. The first doctor prescribed him an oral decongestant, which worked great! He was done with nasal spray forever!

Except the prescription ran out and Ralph's nose went right back to its previous expectation. And no, OTC oral decongestants made no difference whatsoever.

The second doctor recommended that Ralph try detoxing one nostril at a time. Start by only spraying the right nostril and let the left one detox. Then, when the left one is breathing on its own, stop spraying the right one and let it detox while the left one does the heavy lifting.

This experiment lasted less than 24 hours. The incredible pain of the little Thor squeezing the life force out of his left nostril alone was more than Ralph could take.

By year nine, Ralph had begun to notice the decline in his sense of smell, but he felt it was a small sacrifice in light of his ability to breathe, his ability to function in every other way. This was his life now, and he was resigned to it. He'd done his best to hide it, though he figured Desiree was aware, at least to a small degree. It was very hard to hide anything from Desi.

And now Annie.

And Annie appeared to be taking it in stride. Once Ralph seemed to be getting some relief from the bottle she brought him, she went to his kitchen and started fussing around. He could hear the pans and plates clinking, the fridge being opened and closed, cabinets bouncing on their hinges. When he finally felt almost fully human again and wandered into the kitchen, she was creating a generous skillet of stir-fried veggies.

"You don't have soy sauce," she said in greeting, "but this steak seasoning works great on anything. You want Tabasco? I'm a big Tabasco girl."

"Yes. Tabasco," Ralph replied. "There's some in the cabinet there."

As Annie applied the final ingredient, Ralph stood, amazed, wondering how she found all this stuff in his kitchen. He supposed the vegetables had all been in his freezer or canned in his cabinets, but he never would have seen the hodge-podge of packages as a complete meal combination…but this looked fantastic. He could almost smell it.

While they ate, Annie updated Ralph on Joey's condition. He had indeed been moved from the ICU to a regular room and disconnected from the anesthetic that was keeping him asleep. At about four o'clock that afternoon, he had begun showing signs of waking up, and that's when Annie had come to find Ralph and help him out of his own stupor.

"I don't suppose he said anything worthwhile? I mean, about the attack?"

"No. Not by the time I left. But Dr. Savory had told his family not to start pressing him right away. He said Joey would be groggy, would need time to come to understand where he was and what happened. We were warned it wasn't a good idea to start interrogating him, but to let him come back to himself slowly and then he would probably let us know when he was ready to talk. It's possible he's reached that point by now."

Each needing to be in their own vehicle, Ralph and Annie agreed to caravan back to the hospital in Mansfield. Annie went back to her apartment for a few minutes, while Ralph splashed some water on his face and put on a fresh shirt.

When they reached the hospital, it was still daylight, as Daylight Savings Time wouldn't end until October 25. This had been a grueling day for both of them, having not slept in two days other than Annie's catnap in Joey's hospital room, and Ralph's disturbed recovery spell in his apartment. Both of them were beginning to feel the kind of euphoria that can lead to either uncontrollable laughter, or uncontrollable tears. It was a tossup which one of them might give in to which of those impulses first.

Joey's entire family was in his room when Ralph and Annie arrived. Annie took the lead.

"Hey, guys..." she began softly, but Joe Sr. interrupted, understanding what was necessary. He put one arm around his wife's shoulder, and the other around his nearest daughter.

"Let's go find something for dinner," he said, "Joey has some things he needs to discuss with Detective James. Let's give them some privacy."

As the Morouse family filed out of the tiny room, Ralph and Annie took their place at the sides of the bed. Joey reached a hand out to Annie, who took it and held it warmly between both of hers.

"I saw..." Joey began with difficulty. His face, tightly surrounded by bandages, was swollen and probably painful.

"What did you see?" Ralph asked softly, measuring his voice to try to sound as though there was no rush, no pressure. Just a casual conversation between a nonchalant man and the only citizen who might know the identity of the killer or killers who were terrorizing his town. But no pressure.

"I saw...just for a second. It was dark..."

Ralph decided to help Joey out. "Don't try to talk," he interrupted kindly. "I'm going to ask you some simple questions, and I want you to move your right hand if the answer is yes, and your left hand for no. OK?'

Relieved, Joey moved his right hand against the coverlet, and Annie released his left.

"First," Ralph began, "Were you attacked by a gang?"

Left hand.

"So…was it a single person?"

Right hand.

Ralph looked up and met Annie's eyes. This was almost unbelievable.

"And you saw this person?"

Right hand.

"Could you describe him?"

Joey's brows furrowed. Left hand.

"You saw the person, but can't describe him?"

Right hand. And then Joey struggled to speak.

"Was…woman…"

"Your attacker was a woman?"

Right hand.

Again, Ralph met Annie's eyes.

"Was it someone you know?"

Left hand.

"Someone you've ever seen before?"

Left hand.

"Can you describe the woman?"

Hesitation. Then, right hand.

"We're going to need you to try to do that, Joey. I know it's hard, but this is so important."

Annie took Joey's hand again, and he struggled to speak. "Was…old…woman. Old but…strong. Looked like…Arnold…in a…a pink…dress."

"Looked like Arnold? Who is Arnold?" Ralph looked up at Annie, but she shrugged.

Joey licked his lips. "Swash…Arnold…Swash…"

"Arnold Schwarzenegger?"

Right hand.

"The person who attacked you was an old woman who looked like Arnold Schwarzenegger in a pink dress?"

Right hand.

Meeting his eye, Annie shrugged again.

"What kind of weapon was old-lady-Terminator using?"

Hesitation. Then, left hand.

"You didn't see?"

Left hand.

"You *did* see?"

Right hand.

Ralph waited. Joey licked his lips.

"Was…boom…boom."

"Boom boom?"

Left hand. Joey rolled his eyes in frustration.

Ralph patted the bed rail. "Joey, I'm going to let you get some rest. I'm sure I'll have more questions for you. I mean, I really don't understand what you've told me so far…" (Joey raised his right hand) "…and I guess you don't understand it either. But until we solve this crazy thing, you're my main man…OK?"

Right hand.

Ralph looked up at Annie again. "You staying?" he asked.

She nodded.

"Joey, make her go home soon…she hasn't slept since it happened. She's been here the whole time."

Joey raised his eyes up to Annie's face, then moved his right hand.

Ralph was tempted to call Hogan House just to check in and leave a message for Desi if she wasn't still there, but he knew that his mandate for Annie to get some sleep had to apply to himself as well, and he also knew that Desi would agree. If he called in, he might get sucked in, and he would be no use to anyone if he didn't close his eyes for at least a couple of hours. He stepped out into the night breeze and aimed the Sable for home.

Driving down the dark highway back to Cotton Gorge, Ralph had no difficulty staying awake, even though he knew, forensically, that he was exhausted in every way that a human being can experience. His mind was occupied by the oddities of Joey's revelations.

The killer was not a gang, as both Mike Dissart and Dr. Savory had predicted, nor was it a single man. According to Joey, it was a woman. And not just a woman, but an elderly woman…an elderly woman who looked like Arnold Schwarzenegger. Ralph could not wrap his mind around this idea. What could that possibly mean? And the weapon she had used to make the terrible all-over cuts on both Joey and Carmilla…boom boom? An explosive device of some sort? Maybe like a dirty bomb could explode and cause that kind of damage…but that would mean there had been an explosion, which would mean there would be some kind of evidence of an explosion and its aftermath. A mess to clean up. Bits and pieces of shrapnel.

Ralph shook his head again. He knew exactly what Mike would say. The homogeneity of the innumerable lacerations on both Joey and Carmilla ruled out the randomness of exploding shrapnel.

So what did "boom boom" mean?

As Ralph pulled into the drive in front of his apartment, his eye was drawn to the window next door. Mrs. Perkins apartment appeared utterly dark, and he hoped that meant she had been taken into the care of her daughter. He winced a little when his eye fell on the naked twig sticking out of the ground…the sad remainder of her beloved willow tree. How painful it must be to get old and lose your grip on all the things that you once took for granted, even to your basic ability to process the nuances of reality and your own feelings.

He wondered then how this thought correlated to Joey's description of the elderly woman who attacked him. He pictured again Mrs. Perkins as she had ripped up her little tree, struggling with all the strength in the thin, frail muscles of her paper-brittle arms to wrest the little twigs from their root. Mrs. Perkins could not have wielded a flyswatter against a summer mosquito and hoped to cause any noticeable damage.

Ralph knew he had to acknowledge that Joey was still heavily medicated and that his answers may be significantly more intelligible tomorrow…or the next day. But by then, how many more bodies would there be?

Ralph always had a very rigid bedtime routine. He had a drawer full of boxers and t-shirts that were washed with his favorite fabric softener, and these were his pajamas. He didn't wash his other clothes in the fabric softener, because he wanted his sleep clothes to be special. Both the softness and the April Fresh scent had long indicated to his brain that it was time to slow down and go to sleep. Every night he took off his professional clothes and either hung them up neatly for another day or tossed them in the non-pajama hamper for washing. From his pajama drawer, he chose and donned a tshirt and boxers. Then he brushed his teeth and flossed. One should always floss so that one could still have his own teeth when one was ninety. The last piece of his bedtime routine was the final fix: two snorts of oxymetazonline hydrocloride in each nostril, no matter how long it had been since his last dose. This final dose was, ostensibly, to get him all the way to morning without needing to get up for another.

But tonight, Ralph did none of those things except for the nasal spray. He kicked off his shoes, tossed his jacket over the back of a chair, shot himself twice in each nostril, and fell into bed in his clothes. Surely one night without flossing wouldn't cost him his pearlies. At this point, Ralph hardly cared. Some of the greatest people in history had dentures. He pictured himself standing in a room that was always winter, and smiling with teeth made of sparkling snow. Across his snow-teeth ran a tiny row of wire, like the braces he had worn as a teenager, only no…this was a perfect little railroad track, and Ralph could feel the tiny train carrying all the happy people to Christmas town while Rudolph watched kindly from the corner. Ralph resisted the urge to run his tongue across the train track on his teeth…and then he was fully asleep.

When his alarm went off, Ralph reached without opening his eyes and pounded and pounded and pounded on the clock beside his bed, but the penetrating assault of ringing kept on incessantly. Finally awake enough to open his eyes, Ralph realized his alarm had not gone off, because he had not set it the night before, and the noise that wouldn't stop was his telephone.

"Ralph, I'm sorry…I know you were sleeping."

"It's OK, Desi…what is it?"

"There's been another one, Ralph. A body found in the McGuffee field. Chili's on his way, but I knew you'd want to know."

"Any ID?" Ralph was now fully awake and sitting up.

"Woodson said it's Marcus Rath, one of the guys he hired for temporary seasonal work…you know, with the Magical Pumpkin Patch."

"A local?"

"No. Just temporarily. He was staying long-term at the LaDonna through the month of November."

Within eight minutes, Ralph was in his car and roaring at seventy miles an hour through the 30 mph Lake Zone. Adrenaline pumping in rhythm with the revolution of his blaring siren, Detective James couldn't help hoping that the connection between the LaDonna guest and the LaDonna night clerk might be the break he needed to make sense of this nonsensical serial killer.

Chapter Thirteen

New London Texas is a very small town. It's the sort of town where people might say, "Blink, and you'll miss it." But for anyone driving through New London, the one un-missable thing is the enormous monument right in the middle of the street downtown.

In 1937, New London was a booming oil town. A lot of people were making a lot of money, and migrant oil workers came from all over the country to try to get in on the fortune. In order to accommodate all of the children of the oilfield workers, the New London city planners built something they were very proud of: a state-of-the-art school to accommodate all grades of children. It was an E-shaped building, one long structure with three wings branching off from it…one building to house all of the classrooms. The school was a real show of New London's newfound wealth, boasting to be the only school in that half of the state with electric lights on the football field.

But in what might have been the arrogance of wealth, the city planners made one fatal mistake. They chose to heat the school illegally with the natural gas being pumped off of the oilfield. Because this was illegal, it was also unregulated, and in March of 1937, a leak allowed natural gas to begin slowly filling the crawlspace under the school building. It is commonly known that natural gas, in its natural state, has no odor whatsoever, and it was because of this tragedy that the strong sulfur odor began to be added as a warning sign of a gas leak.

But on March 18th, 1937, there was no warning.

There are countless stories to be told of that day, one of which is the story of two brothers, Andris and Sandor, strong sons of

Hungarian immigrants who had made their way to Texas with the dream of finding their fortune in the oil boom. On March 18th, Andris, the older boy, didn't want to go to school. He was feeling sick. There are many stories of children staying home sick that day…after all, they had been unknowingly exposed to the natural gas leak for some time…but Andris's mother made him go anyway. It was a regular school day, everyone excited about and preparing for a big inter-scholastic sport meet the next day in Henderson.

That event never happened.

At 3:17 in the afternoon, as students were getting ready to go home, the shop teacher turned on a belt sander, and the spark ignited the gas. The entire structure of the beautiful New London school lifted off of its foundation, and came crashing back down, burying its victims in a mass of concrete and steel.

Mother Francis Hospital in Tyler was set to have its grand opening ribbon cutting ceremony the next day…but instead, they cancelled the ceremony and opened their doors for the victims. All over East Texas, hospitals, schools and warehouses served as morgues, and in the days that followed, desperate families went from one to the other hoping to find, hoping *not* to find, their children.

Modern visitors to the museum in New London can see a timeline of the rescue effort, in the dark, in the mud because it rained and rained that night. The museum shows newspapers from around the world grieving the tragedy, even a telegram from Adolf Hitler expressing sympathy and support. The monument there today lists all of the children lost, organized by grade, along with their teachers. 294 names are listed on the monument, but in truth, no one really knows the whole number because so many migrant workers gathered the bodies of their children and went home.

Migrant workers like the Hungarian parents of Andris and Sandor.

When the building exploded, Andris was at the flashpoint, and his story ended there. What remains of his legacy is his name listed among the seventh graders on the monument in the middle of town. Likewise, Sandor is listed among the third graders, but his body was never found.

Because it was the end of the school day, the boys' mother, Maartje, had walked to the school to meet her sons and walk back with them to their family camp on the edge of the oilfield. She was just approaching the school, wondering if Andris was feeling better than he had that morning, hoping he wasn't starting a virus that would run through the whole family in their close quarters, when the explosion rocked the whole area and Maartje was thrown off her feet and into a car on the other side of the street.

She awoke the next day in the hospital, surrounded by other wounded adults and children, and her husband was waiting to tell her the news: they were suddenly, tragically, childless.

This wasn't, however, exactly true. The other family survivor that day was the baby girl growing quietly in Maartje's womb, so quietly that Maartje and her husband were not even aware of her yet and would not be for some weeks. Before the new baby had made her presence known, the Hungarian couple had left the nightmare that was New London, and had resettled themselves in Monroe, Louisiana where Maartje's husband found work in construction. By the time Maartje was ready to give birth, the couple had settled into a cozy little house where they would live out the rest of their lives.

When their daughter came noisily into the world, the couple counted their blessings rather than their losses…and named her Desiree, which simply means "desired."

Two years later, they welcomed another daughter, Raine, and the Ligety family was complete. Desiree and Raine were raised with intense expectations, a fierce love, and a constant reminder of the brothers they had never known.

Desiree grew up with a strong feeling of the need to make up for the loss of Andris and Sandor. This wasn't something she could articulate, or even understand within herself, but it manifested in a constant attitude of helping, of leaping to action in the face of any need or any lack on the part of her parents. She worked intently to get good marks in school, and then hurried home, anxious to take on projects that would make the home more orderly and relieve any burden that her mother might feel. No matter what else she might be doing or thinking or wanting in any moment, if Desiree perceived that her mother was in any way unhappy or inconvenienced or tired, she immediately became the busiest bee, dusting shelves that hadn't accumulated any dust since her last dusting, hand-washing clothes that had barely been worn, scrubbing and scrubbing the dishes that were unused since their last washing. Whether the work needed doing or not, the work was her mission.

Raine was a different child. Aware of the tragedy that had stricken her family, she didn't feel the connection that Desiree did. Raine was not so devoted to her schoolwork as her sister, but she put all of her youthful energy and passion into her mastery of the old piano her father had bought for her. While Desiree polished knick-knacks and organized the books and records alphabetically, Raine pounded the keys, playing the same classical phrases over and over until she got them right. The combined determination of the Ligety daughters filled the house with life and vibrance.

By the time she was eight, Raine Ligety began to participate in local area talent competitions…and she was almost always the winner. Desiree did her best to be happy for her prodigy sibling, but it wasn't as easy as she tried to make it look. The day came when Raine received more than just recognition: she was gifted a prize after winning a talent competition at the First Baptist Church of West Monroe, a crisp five-dollar bill.

This was the breaking point for Desiree, and the following day, she threw herself across her mother's bed in an agony of tearful self-loathing. "I don't have any talent!" she wept pitifully, wondering why she had even been born when, clearly, all her parents needed was the shining daughter, Raine, leading them all to the promised land with her heavenly piano fingers.

Maartje, compassionately understanding how her older daughter felt, caressed Desiree's back as it heaved and sobbed, and said, "That's not true, darling. You are the most organized little girl I have ever known!"

Desiree stopped sobbing and sat up abruptly, glowering at her mother. "Oh, yes," she said sarcastically, "I can just hear it now: Ladies and Gentlemen, please welcome our next contestant to the stage. Here is Desiree Ligety, and she is going to…ORGANIZE SOMETHING FOR US! YAY!!!"

Desiree had an incomplete definition of the word "talented," thinking that a *talent* had to be something which could be displayed in a *talent show* like the ones Raine performed in, but in truth, Desiree really was the most organized little girl her mother had ever known, and this only increased as she grew older. By age sixteen, Desiree— now utterly without jealousy for her beloved younger sister—was working as a teller at the First National Bank of West Monroe on Natchitoches Street, and she had already been promoted to supervisor. Even the much older, much more experienced bank employees recognized in Desi a kind of resolute take-charge attitude, coupled with unquestionable trustworthiness.

But when Webb Pierce came into the bank in September of 1955, he didn't see any of that. What he saw was a cute blonde with a ponytail and red lipstick. He leaned casually on Desi's counter, slid his paycheck across it and waited for her to be impressed.

She wasn't.

Accustomed to women seeking his attention, Webb was baffled by Desiree's indifference. Determined to make her smile only for him, he began finding opportunities to hang around the bank, leaning on her counter when there were no customers, and wheedling at her to have dinner with him.

Secretly enjoying the attention, Desi couldn't help noticing Webb's wavy black hair and broad smile. Still, his colorful fashion made her raise an eyebrow, and she wasn't sure any of this was quite appropriate. Just barely seventeen, Desi still held to her parents' values, which would have seen the young man asking her father's permission to date his daughter before boldly approaching Desi herself.

Even so, she found herself watching the front doors of the bank every day, wondering if Webb would come, and secretly practicing her cool responses to his warm intensity.

One afternoon, Webb came only long enough to bring Desi a bouquet of flowers and a big smile. He passed the flowers across her counter and waggled his thick black eyebrows at her, then spun on his heel and walked out as swiftly as he'd walked in. As he pushed through the glass door leading out onto Natchitoches street, Raine Ligety was coming into the bank to bring her sister some lunch. Webb held the door open for Raine, and her eyes grew to twice their regular size as he nodded at her and went out into the street.

Raine glided to Desi's station. "Do you know who that was?" she asked, almost dreamily.

"Yes," said Desiree, not looking up. "A very annoying bank customer."

"That was Webb Pierce!" Raine exclaimed. "*THE* Webb Pierce! Right here! Oh my gosh he held the door for me!"

Now Desiree looked up. What was her sister so excited about? "Do you know him?"

"Know him? Of course I know him! Everybody knows him! Why, his record has been number one practically all *year*!"

Having been much more focused on her future and her career, Desiree had not devoted herself to the study of popular culture the way her sister had. Every night, she could hear the strains of music that squeaked under Raine's bedroom door, emanating from her Mickey Mouse suitcase record player, but this was only a slight annoyance, like a fly buzzing against a windowpane, interrupting Desiree's reading.

At fifteen, Raine was going through an awkward phase, all knees and elbows, and she was conscious of Desiree's classic femininity in a way that Desiree was not. Desi wore her beauty in a careless way, only interested in fashion to the extent that it allowed her to be respected by her peers. Desi did not think of herself as beautiful, nor did she care. Webb Pierce had not been the first man to show her attention, but his persistence coupled with his overtly masculine attractiveness had taken her further into interest than she had been with any previous would-be suitor.

Learning from Raine that Webb was more than just an average man on the street piqued that interest, and Desi was willing to actively seek to know more about her admirer.

That night, Desiree stood with her hands on her hips in the middle of Raine's bedroom listening to a 45-rpm recording of "In the

Jailhouse Now," the chart-topping record that Raine and her peers had been drooling over since December of 1954.

Desi found it to be an utterly ridiculous song, and even worse, badly sung. She could not have borne a second hearing.

Desiree was spared having to have this discussion with the erstwhile Mr. Pierce, because the bank manager called her in the next day to say there was an opening for an assistant manager at a small branch in Cotton Gorge, and Desiree had been recommended. Desi left that very evening to grasp this opportunity, an opportunity which lasted three days before she was sweet-talked into changing careers and taking on the Cotton Gorge Police Station instead. It was something entirely new to sink her creatively organizational teeth into, and Desiree couldn't resist.

In 1958, when Webb Pierce released his song "Cryin' Over You," Raine clipped and mailed Desi a *'Teen* magazine article where Webb was quoted as saying he wrote the song for a "pretty little bank teller" who broke his heart in his hometown. Desi felt obligated to listen.

She found it to be an utterly ridiculous song, and even worse, badly sung. She could not have borne a second hearing.

The simplicity of Cotton Gorge felt tailor made for Desiree Ligety. The experience of moving away from her parents and her friends and starting over in a whole new world was exactly what she had needed without ever knowing she had needed it…and Cotton Gorge needed her even more. Thrilled with the task, Desi took on the years of absolute mess that had collected in the tiny building that was the Cotton Gorge PD, and she worked the kind of magic she'd been born to do, turning a horribly disorganized, lost-beyond-the-possibility-of-redemption public department into an everything-in-its-place environment where all records were pristinely kept, logically labeled and organized into uniform boxes and folders. That aura of trustworthiness that she had taken for granted previously became an obvious boon as the townfolk openly accepted the newcomer and placed their faith in her ability to remember their needs and dispatch help and, most important of all, not tell their secrets.

The passage from girlhood to womanhood isn't as apparent in an old soul like Desiree. To the residents of Cotton Gorge, she was like Athena, born fully formed and already complete and sentient in every way. If they knew she was seventeen upon her arrival in the town, it didn't impact their reception of her. As Desi grew into her full maturity, the town comfortably moved into allowing her a maternal influence on everything and everyone. Desi evolved along with her role, and if she was aware that the maternal role went against any possibility of marriage and family of her own, she never acknowledged it.

The closest Desiree Ligety came to a true maternal relationship began on an evening in 1961 when she was working late, cleaning up the books, and the phone on her desk rang. On the other end of the line was Jenny Farmer, a young woman who had lost the town's support when she began showing all the signs of pregnancy, coupled by none of the signs of matrimony. Jenny was put out by her parents and suffered her pregnancy alone, while working hard labor at the paper mill.

On the night in question, Jenny called the PD hoping Desi would answer. Jenny didn't know Desi personally, but even so, she trusted that this was the person who would help her. Jenny had gone into labor, and she felt like it was happening fast. She had no one else to call and did not believe she would make it to the hospital.

Without even locking the door of the PD building behind her, Desi hurried out into the night and, armed with only the little information she had heard of the process, singlehandedly (and tearfully) delivered Jenny's baby boy, Charles.

Charles Farmer came into the world at an extreme disadvantage. There was no place for an illegitimate child in small town Louisiana. As Desiree held little Charlie (a name he altered to "Chili" in his toddler babble) she could see down the long road before him like an immutable prophecy...and she was determined to be the agent to change it.

From that moment, Desiree took every opportunity to lift up Jenny and Chili, to be certain that the whole town could see how she valued them such that, in time, that value would spread to cover the sin to which the two were originally tethered. Every year, Desi hosted an elaborate birthday party for Chili, and she repeatedly pushed Jenny into positions of local leadership. It seemed an obvious tactic, but it worked. By the time Chili started school, he wore no labels that set him apart from the other children.

Perhaps despite Desi's efforts, and perhaps in part because of them, Chili grew into a wild weed of a teenager. He began making mischief wherever he went, the kind of mischief that was utterly unnecessary. He stole not because he needed anything but because it was fun to see what he could get away with. He drank not to escape worldly problems but to better underscore antisocial behavior like stealing things he didn't need. He made as much noise as he could in the quietest parts of town just to see who might hear him.

The first time sixteen-year-old Chili spent the night in the Hogan House holding cell, Desi stayed all night, napping at her desk. The second time, when he was seventeen, she went into the cell with him and read to him from *East of Eden*.

The third time, when he was eighteen, she sat quietly with him all night and asked him the kind of questions he'd never been asked:

Who are you? What do you stand for? What do you stand against? What do you want in life? How do you wish to be remembered?

After that night, things kind of turned around for Chili. He finished high school at the bottom of his class, but he finished…and then he enrolled in the Shreveport Police Academy. The town was so proud of their native son that no one took notice of the fact that the tuition payments Chili made to the Academy directly correlated with the withdrawals made from Desiree Ligety's savings account.

Chili Farmer graduated the Police Academy at the bottom of his class, but he graduated, and it was only the next natural step when he donned the uniform for the Cotton Gorge Police Department.

It was that smart uniform that caught the eye of Lydia Johnson. Lydia had gone through school a year behind Chili, previously seeing him only as the town troublemaker. The uniform changed that. Chili noticed the shy way that Lydia looked at him when they met by accident in the Piggly Wiggly, and suddenly he saw a woman where previously there had only been a geeky little girl who took school too seriously for his taste.

When he got the courage to ask, Desi smilingly gave Chili the phone number for Lydia's parents and, palms sweating, Chili dialed it. He asked Lydia if she would go out to dinner with him on Saturday night, and she said no. Not wanting to hurt his feelings, Lydia quickly exclaimed that she didn't want to go out on Saturday night because she was deeply devoted to her church activities on Sunday morning, which began early. Undaunted, Chili suggested that perhaps he could simply accompany Lydia to church on Sunday.

At this, Lydia hesitated. "I don't know if that's a good idea," she said. "It's a Pentecostal church. Have you ever been to a Pentecostal church?"

Chili smiled broadly into the phone. "Yes I have!" he assured her. "My aunt Bobbie is Pentecostal, and I've been to church with her a hundred times!"

Reassured, Lydia accepted this plan, believing it would be the best way to bring "the new Chili Farmer" into her parents' purview. On Sunday morning, he showed up in a tidy suit and tie at the Maranatha Fellowship Pentecostal Church, and Lydia led him to their family pew.

The sermon didn't bother him one way or the other. Chili wasn't one for sermons, but he didn't mind other people liking them. What got his attention was when the sermon ended and Lydia's mother stood up and begin speaking in tongues (not that Chili knew to call it this), which sparked like wildfire and soon it seemed like the whole congregation was on its feet, shouting gibberish and falling on the floor. Wide eyed, Chili turned to Lydia, one of very few people not participating in the spontaneous circus, and said, "I just remembered. My aunt Bobbie isn't Pentecostal…she's Presbyterian."

Six months later, Chili and Lydia were married, and eight months after that, their son Jake was born, followed by Jennifer, Jody, and Jeremy. Desiree set herself up as honorary grandmother, a role Jenny Farmer was happy to share with her oldest and dearest friend.

In early October of 1987, Desiree Ligety was a month away from her fiftieth birthday. Her place in the Cotton Gorge community and in the hearts of its residents was secure and unquestioned, and she felt the same about every one of them. In her thirty years in this town, there had never been anything like the killing spree that was taking place that autumn, and Desi was utterly helpless to bring it to an end. Putting down the telephone that Friday morning, after telling Ralph about the body in Woodson McGuffee's corn, she put her hands over her face and hung her head in the kind of misery that can only be felt in true helplessness. Desi was used to having an answer, to having an idea, to knowing how to help in any situation...but now she was just lost. Who would be next?

Two hours later, the kitchen door opened, and Annie Laurie Cherry came inside. Desi did her best to brighten her appearance and be helpful. "How can I help you?" she asked.

"I need to see Ralph...Detective James," Annie said. "I know he's not here. I heard about the new victim, but I need to talk to him as soon as he gets back. It is OK if I just wait here?"

Not only was it OK, but it was exactly the relief that Desiree needed. Bustling about to make fresh coffee and concentrating on idle chit-chat gave Desi permission to stop picturing the mutilated human remains of the various people that she knew and loved.

When the door burst open again just after three o'clock to admit Ralph and Chili, both women dropped to their chairs to wait for the update. Ralph tossed his car keys noisily on Desi's desk.

"It's bad," he said simply.

"It's worse than bad," Chili corrected. "That dude is hamburger meat. He's not even a fat guy, but there's bubbles of fat coming up out of every hole, and there's too many holes to count. I guess he shaves his head...shaved his head...because there weren't no hair on either side, so you can't even tell where his face used to be. Damn."

"That's enough, Chili," Ralph said quietly. "I think these ladies understand how bad it was without the graphic novel version."

Chili wandered back to his office and Ralph continued the narrative that had been interrupted.

"It's bad," he said again. "Mike's guys took him to the lab, but it's obviously the same thing, the same person. Just cut up all over

137

like nothing I've ever seen. I hoped the fact that Marcus was staying at the LaDonna meant he was somehow connected to Carmilla, but I can't find it. Looks like she checked him in a week ago, but otherwise no contact and nothing in common. One of the other workers said Marcus had dinner at the Possum Hole Monday night, but that doesn't connect him to Joey in any way other than just circumstantial. In a small town, everybody's bound to meet everybody at some point."

The mention of Joey's name jarred Annie from her reverie of abject horror.

"Ralph," she said, standing. "I went back to see Joey again this morning and he's much more lucid, much more communicative. That's why I came. I need to tell you some of the things he said."

Annie reached into the back pocket of her jeans and withdrew a folded piece of notebook paper. Unfolding it, she began translating the notes she had scribbled. "OK. He told me how it happened. He said he was leaving my apartment headed for his truck, when a car pulled up, blocking him in. As he moved toward the car, she got out, this old lady in a pink button-up house dress. He said at first, he thought she was fat, but as she moved closer to the light, he realized that she was super muscular. He said her neck and her arms looked like…"

Ralph interrupted to say in tandem with Annie, "…Arnold Schwarzenegger."

"Right!" Annie continued. "So, before he noticed this, he thought maybe she needed help. I mean, anyone would think that. That's why he walked toward her. Then he saw all the muscle and stopped walking, but that's when she started walking toward him, and he said she was hissing like a snake. She said something about "all you vermin are alike" and she was hissing…and then she hit him."

"Hit him with what?"

"With a broom!"

Boom…boom…that wasn't "boom-boom" but instead Joey's tranquilized attempt to say *broom*. Her weapon was a broom.

But that made no sense either. How could anyone do so much damage with a broom?

Reading Ralph's expression, Annie joined in the confusion. "Joey doesn't understand it either. She hit him once, and…lights out."

"Well," Ralph sighed, running a hand through his own tousled hair, "I guess that does answer one thing. Makes sense now why the victims have hay in their wounds. It's not hay from the ground, it's straw from the murder weapon."

Somehow, answering this part of the mystery didn't make anyone feel any better.

Annie turned the paper over in her hands. "Wait! I almost forgot! Joey said her car was a 1959 Caddy with big fins, and even in the dark, he's pretty sure it was pink. He called it "Pepto-pink."

Now it was Desiree's turn to suddenly stand.

"Oh my god, Ralph," she said, her hand flying to her chest as though to quiet the rapid beating of her heart. "Oh my god, I know who it is."

Chapter Fourteen

It was Monday, early morning, and Mamaw was still working on her craft project. She had been up all night long, perfectly sustained by her Manilow-centric nap the day before.

And what a nap it had been. She couldn't remember when she had felt so very good. As she threaded her needle for the thousandth time, she noted that her focus on the tiny eye and the tiny thread was as perfect as when she was twelve years old. Maybe better. She took another moment to pay attention to the sounds around her; she could hear the hum of the refrigerator, the clink of the windchimes in the tree outside, the thin buzz of a housefly in the kitchen…these were sounds she hadn't been able to register for decades.

Her suddenly acute auditory faculties had been of great help last night when Mamaw came home from the store with her bags of craft supplies. She had put the heavy bags on the table and as soon as the crinkling of brown paper subsided, she heard it. The other sound.

The chewing.

It didn't take her more than a second to find where the sound was coming from. Maybe she knew it instinctively, and maybe it was because her hearing, like her vision, was rejuvenated to a point she wasn't even sure she'd had in her youth.

The chewing was coming from the hole in the floor. The Nose was back and was working steadily to enlarge the hole it had begun. Whereas making the beginnings of the hole had required The Nose to chew up from the bottom of the trailer, now that the hole was big enough for The Nose to fit into, it was making quick business out of the augmentation of its portal into her world.

Mamaw stood quietly for a moment, watching the visible whiskers busily feasting on her floor. The hole was much larger now. It had been the size of her big toe when she first found it, but now she could see almost the whole face of the invading creature when he turned just right in his chewing.

She didn't feel the kind of panic or fear she had experienced earlier that afternoon. Just curiosity. She sat down on her favorite spot on the sofa and watched it for a while. Industrious little critter. What did he expect to accomplish? Mamaw didn't watch for long, though because, as late as it was, and as big as the hole was already, she really needed to get started on her project.

Before she stood up, she slipped her foot out of her house shoe and looked at the place where she had been bitten. It was almost completely healed now, even though the bite had only happened about twelve hours earlier. There was a time in her life when a wound of any kind on her foot would have meant weeks of treatment by a doctor who would scold her for her carelessness and warn her repeatedly that diabetics often lost their feet when they didn't take care of them.

There was a time in her life when she would have been terribly afraid of the medical consequences of being bitten by a wild animal, having spent a lifetime reading articles and watching documentaries about such things, about all the kinds of issues that could happen to deter the human body from its natural path of wellness. There was a time in her life when every conversation resulted in an "organ recital" …a methodical recital of all of the things going wrong or possibly going wrong with her various organs.

That time in her life had ended about twelve hours earlier.

The bags of groceries had been heavy. In her previous life, Mamaw would have had to bring each one into the house separately, fighting her way up the steps of her trailer, straining to get the bag to the table, and taking a break between trips to the car to gather her strength. But tonight, she lifted both the bags in her arms at once, held them tight against her body, and had no difficulty climbing the steps. This was slightly surprising, because even getting the bags from the store into her car had been at least a little more difficult. Things were improving.

Before starting her project, Mamaw felt the sudden need—a need she hadn't felt in over twenty years—to look in the mirror. The only mirror remaining in her trailer was the one on the wall in the guest bedroom, and so she opened the door to that lonely room and flipped on the light. The image that greeted her from the silvery surface was…interesting. Mamaw saw her own face, older than she liked to reckon with, but familiar in every way. Her hair was, to put it nicely, questionable. Once long and soft and warm chocolate brown, it was now a steely grey, cropped short and unmanageably wiry. Some women her age had hair that was soft and wispy and white, but not Mamaw. Her hair was like a collection of loose iron filings that had settled on top of her head, like rusting pins on a magnetic pincushion, going in every direction without any ability to coordinate.

Her soft wrinkled cheeks might have made her sad on another day, but tonight she just observed them forensically. These wrinkles were the reward of her eighty years. Each one represented some memory long forgotten. The day she was born, when the midwife spanked her fresh pink bottom, those first tears had begun the formation of the wrinkles looking back at her now. Every moment of pain, every moment of joy, every moment of loss or laughter or love or longsuffering…these moments were all etched into her face like the latitude and longitude lines of the life she had lived. She didn't regret any of them. In those lines were her childhood shelling peas and shucking corn, her wedding day with Papaw, the births of her children, the births of her grandchildren, the long nights up with a colicky baby or a toddler with an earache or a husband with cancer. She wouldn't alter any of them.

But below the face with its map of her world, she saw something utterly unexpected. She remembered her friend Myra saying once that no matter how well-kept a woman's face may be, no matter how much money she spent on night creams and sunscreen, you could always tell her age by her neck. Over the many years since Mamaw was in her forties, she had watched the trim, taut skin of her neck slowly droop down in layered sheets like the *MacArthur Park* cake that someone had left out in the rain, all the sweet green icing flowing down…

But her neck was a melting cake no more. Instead, it was a thick, ripply mass of muscle almost as wide as her head. The skin was stretched tight across the beefy tendons beneath it, such that any sign of the wrinkles that were there yesterday had been erased simply by the strain of encapsulating the freshly grown brawn. She reached up to touch the surprising newness of her neck and was surprised all over again.

Her arms, which had sagged sadly for as far back as she could remember, were now utterly swollen with the kind of muscle reserved for iron-pumping Olympic wannabes. Prominent blue veins popped and throbbed when she flexed her arm in the mirror as she had seen men do on TV. The seam of her sleeve strained as she flexed, and she heard two tiny stitches pop.

All of this was startling in that it had been unanticipated, but in no way was Mamaw upset by her metamorphosis. She could only assume she had The Nose to thank for her transformation, and she would express her thanks in exactly the perfect way, as soon as she finished her craft project.

Returning to the kitchen from the guest bedroom, Mamaw paused once more, just briefly, to check the progress of The Nose as it made its way steadily, and with determination, from its own world into hers. Chewing, chewing, chewing on her floor, gradually enlarging the hole. She looked at the clock and realized that this nocturnal creature would likely be able to fit through his aperture by sunrise, and she would need to have made major progress on her craft by then.

With very little effort, Mamaw lifted the recliner from its ordained spot beside the sofa and carried it to the dining table. The kitchen light was so much better, and besides, she didn't want to disturb The Nose as it worked. From the paper bags she had brought from Piggly Wiggly, she withdrew and counted out the eight boxes of 100-count razor blades. Eight hundred razor blades. She really needed about two thousand, but eight boxes had been all they had in stock.

She stacked the boxes neatly into two little towers, opened the first box and removed one of the shiny little rectangles. It was so pretty, the way it reflected the overhead light and then cast the reflected light onto the wall of the trailer. Mamaw adjusted her hold on the blade and threw the light all around herself like a disco party. Holding the tiny blade up to the light, Mamaw peered through the perfectly circular hole in the middle of the rectangle. She knew that pushing the needle through the straws of her broom would be taxing but getting it through that hole in each of the eight hundred razor blades would be absolutely cathartic.

And so she began. Using the extra sturdy hand-quilting thread, Mamaw speared the needle through the end of one of the thousands of straws in her favorite old broom, anchored the thread with a close knot, then looped the needle through the hole in the razor blade, and drew it tight. She tied off another knot and clipped the thread with her tiny gold pelican scissors.

It was perfect. Only seven hundred ninety-nine to go.

At five-seventeen Monday morning, the chewing noise stopped. Mamaw paused in her work, looking down at the five empty razor blade boxes at her feet, and decided this was fine. The craft project wasn't finished, but it was finished enough to welcome her guest. Mamaw turned in her chair to peer at the hole in her living room floor, just in time to see the nose emerge, followed laboriously by the entire body of her invader, the invader who never got past the sofa.

The first time she had hit The Nose with her broom, the previous day, she had scared it away, but in doing so, she had utterly exhausted herself. This time there was no exhaustion, only the incredibly therapeutic swishing swishing swishing of her broom, the chime-like clinking of the razor blades attached to the straws, and the unspeakable thrill of the soft *thunks* as the weapons landed, imbedded, and then dragged noiselessly through the flesh of her adversary.

The Nose was motionless after the second swish of her broom, but Mamaw swished the broom at least a dozen more times just for the pure pleasure of it. Once she declared herself finished, she looked down at the shredded beast bleeding on her throw rug and decided she didn't like it there. She rolled the rug up around the disemboweled carrion and hauled it to the bedroom before returning to her project.

Vermin. She wasn't going to let vermin take over her life. She wasn't going to just sit here in her trailer and wait for the vermin to come; Mamaw was going to go out there and stop them before they showed up. She worked steadily until all but one of her boxes were empty, and the dawn was as softly pink in her kitchen window as the Cadillac parked in her driveway.

Mamaw was tired. Mamaw was going to sleep all day and then finish her project and begin making her arrangements the following evening.

Mamaw was formulating a plan.

Chapter Fifteen

As he drove, Ralph couldn't help but berate himself for missing this earlier. Mrs. Perkins had tried to tell him, after all. She asked him to check up on her friend Effie who wasn't answering the phone, and if he had, Marcus Rath would still be alive.

Effie Maude Solomon. Desi had been able to identify her immediately by the Pepto-pink 1959 Cadillac.

"Her son Harry bought her that car brand new, but Effie's such a homebody, I'll bet she hasn't put twenty thousand miles on it."

"And the rest of the description sounds like her?" Ralph had asked as he and Chili donned their rarely used Kevlar and gun belts.

"Not the Schwarzenegger muscle part, of course, but the button up pink house dress for sure. The other makes no sense to me. Effie was already a widow when I moved to Cotton Gorge, already seemed like an old lady. I didn't ever have a reason to get to know her very well, but she always seemed so sweet. A genuine Southern Belle."

Chili scoffed. "Well, Miss Scarlett never chopped anyone up for giblet gravy like your friend Effie."

"Effie lives in that little old trailer that you pass when you head out toward the Corbett farm. Bobby and Judy kind of keep an eye on her; sometimes they bring her groceries."

"Looks like they've let down the watch this week," Ralph quipped as he opened the kitchen door.

Ralph and Chili rode in almost silence, which was unusual for Chili especially. His grave speechlessness conveyed his recognition of the import of this trip. In his years since the Police Academy, Chili had dealt with a wide variety of small-town misdemeanors, but never anything like this. He'd watched crime-scene videos and studied cadavers in forensics labs, but from all of that he felt disconnected, like watching a TV show that he could turn off without fearing that it would become real. In the nine minutes that it took to drive from Hogan House to the Corbett place, Chili Farmer grew up.

Ralph had chosen not to drive with sirens blaring. He could have turned it on if slowed down by someone's John Deere on the highway, but that hadn't been necessary, and he didn't want to raise alarm nor alert their octogenarian serial killer with the extraneous noise. This decision ultimately made no difference, because as they pulled into Effie Solomon's gravel drive, they could see immediately that no Pepto-pink Caddy was present.

Without needing to consider his options, Ralph did the thing he never did: he broke down the door of Effie's 1955 Terra-Cruiser. There was no extra key, and no time to knock on the Corbett's door to ask for one. If they were right, Effie wouldn't be coming back to this house anyway, and if they were wrong, Ralph would buy her a new door out of his own paycheck.

That entire thought process took place during the 2.7 seconds that it took for Ralph to raise his right foot, brace himself, and slam the sole of his shoe into the door right beside the ancient doorknob. The door pushed open with barely creak and a sigh of relief. Before entering, Ralph told Chili to walk around the outside of the trailer and make note of anything that stood out as anomalous.

Once inside the stuffy trailer, Ralph gripped his pistol tightly, flipped on the light and called "Police!" No sound greeted him in response, so he holstered his gun and fully entered the small structure.

At first glance around, it looked like any other eighty-year-old woman's house. The mass-produced artwork on the walls was generally faded, mostly showing pastoral landscapes and floral motifs. A few little signs that advertised clichés like "True friends don't knock." Ralph wondered if that made him her true friend. He certainly hadn't knocked.

On the kitchen table was a spool of thread and a Southwestern Bell telephone book. One wall of the dining area displayed a set of four Bradford Exchange china plates showing scenes from The Sound of Music. A 1978 McDonalds coloring book calendar was pinned to the fridge with an alligator magnet. Every page was colored and signed by "Meg."

Ralph walked across the room, past the sofa, to the large wooden stereo console against the wall. Atop the stereo was a little mono cassette player, and beside that was a stack of three cassette boxes. The one on top was Barry Manilow's *This One's For You* album, and the photo of Barry that illustrated the entire front of the paper insert, in shades of yellow and orange, gave Ralph a moment of pause.

"Sure looks like someone who had to sell his soul for worldly success," Ralph muttered to himself. "That man's got a face for radio."

He turned the cassette over in his hand and then looked up as Chili stepped inside.

"I don't see anything out of order in the…" Chili cut himself off with an exclamation. "Holy Catholic testicles! What the hell is that smell??"

Ralph, having smelled nothing out of the ordinary, just stood stark still as Chili dashed from the room to the back of the trailer and then called again.

"Judas Priest, Ralph…get in here!" he shouted. "It smells like foster-kid casserole in this bedroom!"

Ralph turned away from the console, took two steps, and then his left foot sunk through the throw rug and into the floor, effectively snaring him like a booby trap.

"Chili, I need your help," he called.

Once Chili had freed him from the floor, and Ralph had recovered his left shoe which had remained in the rug-trap when his foot was released, both men went back to Effie's bedroom where the odor was strong enough that Ralph caught a whiff.

He opened the closet, as that would be the most likely place for a body to be hidden, but the closet only revealed a row of cotton house dresses, three pair of sensible shoes and about thirty years' worth of Christmas wrapping paper remainders.

Under the bed, Chili found several torrid romance paperbacks, an empty box of Little Debbie Nutty Bars which appeared to predate the 1980s, and a full box of colorful rhinestone jewelry which perhaps Effie had hoped would come back in style.

Throughout the frenzied search, Chili kept up his ceaseless stream of metaphors for how unbearable he found the smell…and then he discovered its source.

Whipping back the lumpy coverlet, Chili revealed the decomposing carcass of what had, about a week ago, been a rather large opossum. The part of the animal they could see was covered with the same kind of bloody wounds as the human victims in Cotton Gorge, and the part of the animal they couldn't see wasn't there because…

"Jiminy Skywalker," Chili whistled low. "Looks like she killed this poor bugger and has been sleeping with him and eating on him for several days."

Ralph concurred. "I think we've found victim number one," he said. "Get this thing out of the house, Chili."

While Chili bundled the dead marsupial back in it's throw rug to haul him out of the house, Ralph stepped back into the living room. Passing the kitchen trash can, he stooped down to remove an empty box that boasted a hundred razor blades. He quickly counted the seven other boxes and began slowly picturing the engineering these boxes might be evidence of.

Chili came back into the house. "I'm having a thought," he said. Without further explanation, he whipped the McDonalds coloring book calendar off the fridge and began scribbling over the dates of August 1978.

"Yeah…" he said. Then turning back to Ralph, "Yeah! Man, why didn't I see this before?"

Intrigued, Ralph stepped over to read Chili's scribble.

"Look at the names, Ralph…the victims' names! Carmilla Rabbi, Joey Morouse, Marcus Rath."

Ralph looked.

"Don't you see it? Look, if you add a T here, it's RABBIT. If you take away the RO here, it's MOUSE. If you take away the H here, it's RAT."

Ralph kept looking.

"And victim number one was a damn possum!"

Ralph's eyes opened wider as he got what Chili was saying.

"Vermin!" he exclaimed. "She was exterminating vermin!"

Ralph hurried to the kitchen table and picked up the little telephone book, turning to the R's. As he expected, Carmilla's name and address were circled.

"She's looking for vermin! She must've gone a little crazy when that possum came in through the hole…"

And then the full realization hit him. "Oh my god, the Possum Hole. That's her end game! The bloody note…that was possum blood. The lyrics she wrote…"

Ralph rushed back over to the stereo console and picked up the Manilow cassette again. Turning it over in his hand, he read the song titles. What he was looking for wasn't there, but he picked up the next one, the *Barry Manilow II* album, and there it was. The final track on Side A: "Something's Comin' Up."

Ralph looked at his watch. It was after five. Annie would be at the Possum Hole by now getting ready for the Friday night dinner rush. If Effie Maude Solomon meant to do maximum damage in a den of "vermin" this would be the night.

This time with the siren blaring, Ralph and Chili rushed back toward town, hoping to never find out how much damage could be done in one small-town bar by a possum-pumped muscle-bound granny wielding a broom full of razor blades.

Chapter Sixteen

As Annie walked up the road from Hogan House back to the Possum Hole, she noted the crisp autumn air, the only thing in the world that made her feel nostalgic for the cult.

Every year, on the 15th day of the Hebrew month of Tishrei began the Jewish festival of Sukkot, commonly translated as The Feast of Tabernacles. For Christian cults attempting to appropriate the Hebrew calendar, this meant that the Feast could fall anytime in the autumn on the Roman calendar, and the first snap of cool in the air gave Annie the *longings*.

In a life otherwise dictated by ostracism and poverty, the Feast of Tabernacles was for Annie's cult like a week-long Christmas of inclusion. Of course, they didn't openly acknowledge it in those terms, as Christmas—like all other Christian holidays—had pagan origins and was therefore unmentionable in connection with the true Old Testament high days.

One third of the thirty percent of their income that the cult members had to "tithe" all year was set aside in a special account to be spent on the holy days, and this mostly meant the Feast of Tabernacles. For a family of four, even a lower middle-class family of four, to have a full ten percent of their annual income to spend in a single week was like a glimpse of Utopia…which was, in fact, the point of the Feast.

The week of wealth was only part of the glory of this holiday though. The other part was the gathering of cult members from around the world into large pockets of people. Globally, the cult had nearly half a million members, but scattered worldwide, that meant that most people only saw other members on the Sabbath. But for one week every autumn, members gathered into about 90 different "Feast sites," converging on beach towns and ski resorts and, inexplicably, the Poconos. Every place that the cult decided to make a Feast site was a city whose economy would swell enormously during the Feast of Tabernacles, and they were all happy to welcome the members of this weird religion who suddenly had many thousands of dollars in income which was not only disposable, but which *must* be disposed of in this week.

Depending on their location, every family in the cult had an "assigned" Feast site, which was relatively local and the default place for them to spend this eight-day revival extravaganza. In Florida, families might be assigned to Pensacola, or St. Petersburg. In North Carolina, families were assigned to Virginia Beach. Annie would hear about the Feast-goers in Los Angeles or Lake Tahoe or Jekyll Island, all of the "not wise men" who were assigned to celebrate the festival in those exotic places.

The congregation to which the Ward family belonged was assigned to Big Sandy, Texas. Big Sandy, which had a single gas station/convenience store and a hole-in-the-wall hamburger joint and that's all. Well, not exactly all, because Big Sandy had 130 acres of land that belonged to the cult and was utilized as a campground for the annual Feast-ers. For one week of every year, thousands of cult members would converge on that acreage and set up tents or pop up campers or rented motor homes and live all together in ostensible harmony for the duration of the Feast.

Annie Laurie Ward loved the Feast of Tabernacles. She *lived* for it all year. When she and Donny were little the Feast meant, most of all, presents. Her family's tradition was that every morning when Annie and Donny woke up, there would be a wrapped gift on the end of their bed.

Every single morning.

The monumental importance of this to a four, five, six, seven-year-old cannot be overstated. One day might be a coloring book and crayons—the box of 64 with the built-in sharpener—and the next day might be a beautiful new doll. Every year, the level of creativity that Mrs. Ward put into the choosing and distributing of the daily presents was beyond praiseworthy. Every year there were games, there were gifts with batteries, there were gifts to ride on, gifts to make art with, gifts to snuggle, gifts to eat, and gifts to wear.

Among these daily gifts, there were always specific gifts that were ear-marked to be church-toys. Attendance at the church services was a mandatory daily part of the Feast of Tabernacles, but little children—while expected to be quiet—were not expected to pay close attention to the doomsday prophecies that were being shouted daily from the pulpit for two-to-four hours. Instead, Annie and Donny were allowed to take their church-toys into the enormous corrugated steel building that was affectionately called "The Tabernacle" and sit in one of the many thousands of metal folding chairs and play quietly while their parents competed with the other adults to see who could find the referenced scripture faster than their neighbors. Church-toys included Barbie dolls with hair that could be brushed and braided, or a new set of Peanuts Gang Colorforms, or a book of word-find puzzles.

Church-toys never had batteries.

In her teens, Annie began to get in on the Feast gift planning, enjoying the elaborate shopping trips with what felt like endless financial freedom to choose the crafting supplies or specific gifts for friends and family.

But there was much more to the Feast than the gifting. When Annie was a small child, the campsite seemed to just appear out of nowhere, ready to go, and how fun it was to camp! She had a very particular feeling of homesickness that was brought on by the sound of a tent-zipper, which invariably led her to the olfactory sense memory of fresh campfire coffee and sizzling breakfast sausage cooked on an outdoor grill. These Feast mornings were some of her most cherished, and most persistent, recollections.

Feast friendships were also an annual highlight. At the Feast, Annie would be reunited with friends that she only saw just once a year, and what a revelry that would be! Campground sleepovers and the constant plan of who would sit with whom at daily services, sharing new toys with old friends, singing by the campfire at night with several families gathered together…nothing in Annie's later life could ever compare to this.

But Big Sandy Texas in the autumn usually meant something else important and almost unavoidable: rain.

Some years, the rain would choose a day here or a day there to drizzle, and some years, the entire Feast of Tabernacles was utterly drenched in a non-stop downpour. Every camp was wet, every element of Sabbath-Best clothing was damp and mildewing. The long walk from the campground to the Tabernacle saw thousands of people just trudging through mud and trying to keep their families from melting into the soggy landscape.

The Feast when Annie was seventeen, her father set up three tents: one big one for himself and his wife, and two smaller ones for Annie and Donny to each have their own space. The adults' tent was a classic canvas structure with a drooping ceiling leading out to straight walls. Likewise, Donny's tent was a smaller version of this same style structure. Annie's tent, however, was a simple A-frame.

She hated it. When the rain came, as it invariably did, the walls of her tent were so wet with it that she had to move her bed to the very center so as not to touch the mouldering canvas on either side of her. She begged Donny to trade with her. He never had friends stay like she did, and he would be better able to cope with the limited dry space. Donny, of course, had a myriad of reasons why he wouldn't trade with her, and ultimately, he said that he would only trade if Annie would "throw in" her half of the Casio SA-2 electronic keyboard that their parents had given them as a joint Feast gift. Annie honestly considered this offer. It was only the third night of the Feast, and the idea of sleeping in the larger, dryer tent was almost worth half a keyboard.

Thankfully, she decided to "sleep on it" and that night came the deciding element. It rained harder and heavier that night than she had ever known a Feast night to rain, and about midnight, the water that had collected in the drooping roof of her parents' tent became more than the structure could bear…and the whole thing fell. Annie was awakened by the shrieks of her mother as the canvas and the poles and the water came crashing in on them.

Within ten minutes, the same thing happened to Donny's tent. The rainwater had gathered in the saggy parts of the roof, overburdening it until it pulled the tent down with it, and Donny's shrieks were added to those of his parents.

Mom, Dad, and Donny spend the next hour and a half getting their tents back up, and spent the rest of the night wet. Annie, on the other hand, in her A-frame tent where the water ran down the sides rather than pooling in the top, stayed snug under her covers and in the still-ownership of half a Casio keyboard.

The next year, Mr. Ward rented a motor home, but that was the year Annie was married to Dave Cherry and didn't attend the Feast of Tabernacles anymore.

Still, seven years later, when the first nip of fall hit the air, Annie could hear the poetic hum of a tent zipper and smell the campfire coffee and sizzling sausage.

That Friday evening, October ninth, as Annie walked from Hogan House to the Possum Hole, she did a quick calculation and realized that the Feast had already begun. Just then, somewhere in a campground in Big Sandy Texas, her parents were probably starting dinner with old friends, talking about old times, laughing about the year the tents fell…maybe trying to explain, again, where Annie Laurie was.

Perhaps Annie's Christmas room was an attempt to create a new version of that old feeling. She wouldn't ever celebrate the cult Holy Days again, but the little girl in her still desperately wanted that sense of excitement and anticipation. In order to do that, she had to make new memories that fit within the mainstream she had moved into, new memories which at least attempted to rival the old ones. But how can a twenty-five-year-old woman ever manufacture the sublime enchantment of a kindergartner awakening to a wrapped gift at the foot of her camp cot?

She looked up at the moon, which was just visible in the late afternoon sky; it would have been full two nights ago on the eve of the first Holy night of the Feast of Tabernacles.

The Hebrew calendar often correlated its Holy Days with the full moon. Funny, she thought, walking along, how so many other traditions associated the full moon with bad things, monsters, evil and mischief-making.

She thought about Joey lying on her porch, indistinguishably shrouded in his own blood and shredded flesh, displayed beneath Wednesday night's full moon. The Festival moon.

Shuddering, Annie had the thought that Joey's body, in its grisly gift wrap, might be her final and most perpetually memorable Feast gift.

158

She thought then of Joey as he had been that morning in the hospital. Still bandaged and swollen, but laughing, cracking jokes, ordering orange juice. This thought made her start to smile despite all the other difficulty of the day.

And then she heard the sirens.

Chapter Seventeen

Ralph's brain was moving a million miles a minute. Going over and over what Joey had said, he put the pieces of the puzzle together as he drove.

Vermin. Joey said that's what she called him. Joey Morouse, whose name, minus two letters, looked like Mouse. He said she called him vermin, and that she was hissing like a snake.

…hissing like a *possum*.

The possum had started it all. It had invaded her home and sent her on a tear through the town to rid her world of vermin. The image of the rotting, half-eaten carcass on Effie's bed turned his stomach afresh. Ralph wasn't sure he would ever be able to shake that vision. Was Effie's transformation entirely psychosomatic? The muscles, the hissing? Or had eating the butchered possum engendered her physical changes?

Ralph thought about his own grandmother, Ruby. On TV, grandmothers always lived in classic country homes where they wore aprons and baked pies and told stories of the good old days. Gramma Ruby didn't match this description at all. She had lived, to Ralph's recollection, in one falling-down rent house or apartment after another, transiently making her way through life with a nasty old black cat named Rastus. Gramma Ruby had a shelf-full of paperback horror novels with deliciously titillating cover art, and always in her kitchen was an enormous plastic barrel of Cheez Ballz.

When Ralph visited Gramma Ruby, whether in his childhood, or later as an adult, she would welcome him into her falling down rent house or apartment, offer him a seat, and then proceed to talk absolutely non-stop about anything and everything she could think of.

This was, most often, an unending discourse on the various health issues of everyone she knew, almost none of whom Ralph knew, but this didn't matter to Gramma Ruby. She would name-drop thirty people in any given conversation, with no regard to whether Ralph had ever heard of this person. Were they distant relatives? Were they neighbors of hers from five years ago? These irrelevant details had no bearing on Gramma Ruby's telling of the tales and Ralph had learned from infancy not to ask. Just listen.

And so he heard about the person with a mouth ulcer so big the doctors had to remove his tongue. He heard about the lady who had fallen and broken her leg for the fifth time. He heard about babies born sideways and genetic anomalies not discovered until adulthood and shattered hips and cataract surgeries and deadly staph infections and gout. Gramma Ruby offered up the luridly colorful descriptions of gangrenous limbs and emergency amputations and common colds that turned into blood poisoning and exotic parasites brought home from family vacations.

Ralph often wondered what Gramma Ruby's life might have been like if she had associated more frequently with *healthy* people. Perhaps she would have run out of grisly topics and instead gotten a degree in philosophy or business management or dental hygiene.

He could not picture Gramma Ruby doing these things any more than he could picture her as a muscle-bound murderer, feasting on carrion and terrorizing her town.

Somewhere, someone was thinking the same of Effie Maude Solomon. Somewhere were the children and grandchildren represented in her trailer, and they thought of her as a mild-mannered, gracefully aging Southern Belle.

"There it is!" Chili shouted suddenly, breaking Ralph out of his trance. Jolting out of his highway hypnosis, Ralph squinted at the taillights in front of him in the waning afternoon light and could just make out the edges of the Cadillac fins. Pepto-pink.

Preparing for a high-speed chase, Ralph stepped on the gas, and as the Sable jerked forward, throwing Ralph and Chili back against their headrests, the Caddy spurted forward at a faster speed as well. The road was long and straight, and Ralph was certain he could catch her, pass her, and cut her off.

But almost before he had time to react, the Caddy slammed on its brakes and Ralph, moving at about ninety miles per hour, almost slammed into the rear end of her car.

"Jim Beam in a sippy cup!" Chili exclaimed, throwing his hands out to grasp the dashboard. "Why is she stopping?"

"She's not stopping," Ralph said as he felt his internal organs settle back into their pre-appointed places. "She's slowing down for the Lake Zone."

Sure enough, the pink Caddy was now going exactly 30 miles per hour, seemingly oblivious to the siren-screaming Mercury Sable behind it. Somewhere inside the vicious slashing serial-killer was the law-abiding citizen who had been adjusting her speed in respect of the unmanifested Cotton Gorge Lake, the coolest hot spot in Louisiana, since 1967.

This sudden change rather disoriented Ralph as to what to do next. If she was speeding away from him, he would have chased her down, taken the lead, cut her off in a cloud of dust and squalling tires. But at 30 miles and hour, what was the point? For forty seconds— forty long seconds—he just drove behind her like a courtesy police escort, blaring the siren such that there's no way she didn't know he was there. And then she pulled over.

His thought was that she pulled over because of the siren-blaring police car behind her, but then he realized that she had pulled over because she had reached her destination. The Possum Hole Bar and Grill was on the corner at the front of the road leading back to the Hogan House, and Annie Laurie Cherry was just walking to the front door.

When the cars pulled up, Annie turned and took a few steps towards them, as though not registering what was happening. Switching off the siren, Ralph leapt out of his driver's side door and shouted at her. "Annie, stay back!" Dutifully, she froze.

Seemingly unaware of any circumstances beyond her own mission, Effie Solomon was slowly rising out of her own car, pulling with her the broom which had occupied the passenger seat. Paying no mind to Ralph and Chili, who had both drawn their guns and were calling her name, ordering her to freeze, Effie focused her attention on her goal: Annie.

Slowly, she walked around the front of the Cadillac, holding up her broom. With the car no longer between them, she stopped and faced Annie, and began swaying…and hissing.

In that moment, Ralph experienced the purity of a classic moral crisis. If he had found himself standing here facing down a man—say, if Woodson McGuffee turned out to be the killer and now he was threatening Annie—Ralph would have pulled the trigger in the face of this threat. Maybe he would have been cool about it, shooting Woodson in the calf just to bring him down and then reciting his Miranda rights while wondering if the movie version of this might include Robert Redford as the intrepid Detective James.

If the perp in this scenario had been a woman, but a *young* woman, some Bonnie Parker type trying to resolve her own existential questions by gleefully committing murder and mayhem in rural America, well, Ralph would surely have taken her down.

But no, the killer was literally a classic little old lady. A grandmother. Not like his grandmother...the kind who *baked!* How could he shoot her? At her age, a shot in the calf would be the same as a shot in the head. She hadn't meant to be a killer...she was just confused. Hulking and threatening and downright scary looking with all that muscle stretching her shapeless flowered cotton dress...but confused. Confused and probably afraid and thought she was defending herself.

Ralph glanced at Chili and saw the exact same crisis playing out on his face, but as Effie stepped slowly forward, swaying and hissing and raising her broom, Ralph knew he had to act.

In one quick swoop, he reached into the back seat of his car for the only thing he had brought with him from Effie's trailer. Slamming it onto the roof of the Sable, he pushed the PLAY button with all the force of his frustration and the still October night was suddenly filled with the voice of Barry Manilow.

"All the time...all the wasted time...all the years, waiting for a sign!"

Undaunted by the sirens or the commands from the police officers, Effie suddenly froze in her tracks for Barry Manilow.

Turning slowly on her heels she faced Ralph and made eye-contact. Without even thinking about it, he lowered his gun and met her gaze.

For the rest of his life, Ralph James never could find the words to adequately describe the next few seconds of his career as a police detective. Even in the low light of sunset, he could see the tears well in Effie Solomon's eyes, and simultaneous to the welling of tears was the recession, the physical ebbing, of her unnatural musculature. Before his eyes, Effie was deflating, as though the pin prick of the familiar and beloved voice had made its mark not firmly enough to pop the balloon, but to simply allow the air to leak out slowly, but perceptibly, until standing before him was not a murderer on a homicidal spree, but a frightened and decrepit great grandmother who, coming out of a spell of dementia, didn't know where she was.

Gazing at him through her veil of bewildered tears, while Barry continued to sing to the world his cautionary tale of a wasted life, Effie took a step towards Ralph, dropping her broom into the dust by the side of the road, its cache of razor blades glittering in the twilight like early holiday lights. She opened her mouth as though to speak, but instead, her eyes grew suddenly wide and she clutched her chest with both of her withered hands. Uttering one small "Ah!" she crumpled to the ground beside her pink Cadillac.

Chapter Eighteen

He hadn't ever realized the lights would be so bright. Now that he was experiencing it, he totally understood; he just felt like he hadn't been fully prepared.

The one relief in live television was the commercial breaks. About a dozen people were rushing around, adjusting lights and cameras, touching up makeup, straightening various items on the set. The only thing required of Ralph was to sit still and wait…and to be patient with the lady who powdered the shine on his forehead caused by a combination of the bright lights and the general anxiety native to this experience.

He risked a glance out into the dark audience. Right there on the front row sat Annie Laurie Cherry, smiling at him broadly with her perfectly crooked teeth. Ralph wasn't sure he would have been able to pull this off without her support. It was truly amazing to him that he had only known her for about seven weeks, because in that short time she had become such an integral part of his life.

Mrs. Perkins had not come back to occupy her apartment at 3704 Richmond Street. Desiree had never gotten any further news about her condition, and Ralph didn't expect that they would. Ralph and Annie had tripped across her porch every day for weeks now. Ralph kept a toothbrush at Annie's apartment, and Annie had an entire drawer in Ralph's dresser.

Ralph had heard it said that a relationship begun under extreme duress was not likely to last in the long-term. He and Annie had discussed this at length, and ultimately, they decided that "extreme duress" is a relative term. There had definitely been duress throughout the ordeal, but the only extreme they had shared had been at the very end, and that had lasted less than 90 seconds. Separately, they had each experienced "extreme duress"—Annie when she found Joey left for dead on her porch, and Ralph as he dealt with the murders and with the realization of Effie's end game, rushing to the Possum Hole. But they decided their separate instances of "extreme duress" didn't count in the discussion of whether their relationship had begun under those circumstances. They readily admitted that they had shared a mutual attraction from the first meeting, which was—at least almost—free of duress.

Not that a note with Barry Manilow lyrics written in the blood of a slaughtered marsupial wasn't at least a little duress-ful...but they had agreed to downplay that part.

Ralph had been putting his detective skills to a new and interesting venture of late: house hunting. In secret, during time off when Annie was at the Possum Hole, he had been working with a local realtor to find a house where he and Annie could live together. He wanted a fresh start. Something with a big kitchen and at least three bedrooms: one for them, one for company and/or junk storage, and one for Annie's year-round Christmas.

Last week, he had found the perfect place. A new house built in a new subdivision just on the north edge of town. Fresh paint, fresh appliances, fresh start. He had signed the lease yesterday, and the key was in his pocket. He planned to present it to Annie at dinner this very evening. Dinner in New York City.

Annie had already given him a life changing gift. Once Joey was out of the hospital and she could pay attention to other things, Annie had come to Ralph's apartment one Saturday morning with a nasal spray bottle and a larger container of saline.

She explained that the trick was to detox from his addiction without letting his nose know what was happening. "The nasal spray in this bottle," she said, "is already slightly diluted with saline. Go ahead and use it like always, use it whenever you need it, but tomorrow night I want you to open it up and add an eighth of a teaspoon of saline. After that, every two days, add another eighth of a teaspoon of the saline, and I think you'll find you need to dose yourself less and less often."

Skeptical, Ralph was in that early glow of love where he was willing to try anything for Annie's sake, and so he followed these instructions to the letter. He was stunned to find that within a week, he was dosing maybe once every 24 hours, and then within two weeks, he wasn't dosing at all. He was free of the chains that had bound him for thirteen years to the demon that was oxymetazoline hydrochloride.

Joey Morouse was not only released from the hospital but was back working at the Possum Hole. The wear and tear on his body didn't seem to be slowing down his stream of suitors; he was now the Beautiful Young Man with the Mysterious Scars. Earlier that week, he had received a letter from Baton Rouge Community College offering him a full scholarship, including housing, into their Associate of Applied Science in Entertainment Technologies program, beginning in mid-January. Apparently, someone had written them a letter telling Joey's story. Ralph knew it wouldn't take long for Joey to figure out that he and Annie had done that together, but so far, the kid was so swept up in the excitement, he hadn't started asking questions.

Cotton Gorge had all but completely recovered from the murder spree of early October. It had, of course, been all the talk for a while, but then the gossip train changed tracks when the town awoke one morning to these words:

"My people are the people of the dessert," said T.E. Lawrence, picking up his fork.

168

This was painted in purple in the middle of the street in the little downtown area where local shopkeepers sold hand-milled soaps and overpriced children's clothes.

The painted phrase defied explanation, and so of course everyone had to offer their own interpretation, and great debate ensued. After three days, Mayor Josiah Rickards decided the phrase was a traffic hazard, as so many people were standing in the street to study or photograph or otherwise experience the nuances of the words, and so he had a service come from Vivian to sand-blast the painted words off of the asphalt and life could return to normal.

Only the very next morning, the words had been re-painted, this time in red. General opinion was that it was not the same writing style and therefore probably a copycat vandal, but the Mayor had no more money to hire the Vivian sand blasters a second time, and also no confidence that there wouldn't be a third incarnation of the cryptic phrase…so he left it there.

In all the hubbub about T.E. Lawrence and his fork, talk had turned away from the Mamaw Murders (as the Shreveport Times had dubbed the series of attacks), and routine resumed in Cotton Gorge.

Still, the larger world had a more sustainable interest in the Mamaw Murders, which is what ultimately led to Detective Ralph James sitting under the bright lights of a live television studio while a young woman powdered his nose and somewhere from the dark, a director called, "Everyone! In five…four…three…"

"Welcome back, everyone. Thanks for being with us on *Good Morning America*. I'm your host Charles Gibson, and we're chatting with Detective Ralph James from Cotton Gorge Louisiana. You've no doubt heard the sensational story of the Mamaw Murders, and you've heard the name Ralph James, the man who brought the killing spree to an end."

Here, Charlie turned away from the cameras to face Ralph. "Detective James, I'm so glad you were able to join us here today. This story has just been fascinating. What must it have been like trying to solve a murder series like this?"

"It was truly indescribable, Charlie," Ralph said, gauging whether his voice sounded more composed than he actually felt.

"I understand that Marvel Comics has already bought the rights to your story so that they can produce the film version."

"That's right," Ralph agreed, "I'll be credited as a consultant on the screenplay."

Charlie's voice softened and he looked deeply into Ralph's eyes. "I can't imagine how hard it must have been," he said, "there at the end when you had to face down this vicious killer, but also you were just looking at a confused elderly woman."

"It was hard, Charlie," Ralph nodded sadly, remembering. "she looked at me, and she had tears in her eyes. I could tell she was wanting to ask me what was happening, where she was, why she was in the street like that…and then it was too much. Her heart just gave out. I kind of felt like mine did too."

Charles Gibson was silent for a moment, letting that thought sink in for himself and for the audience, and then he reached over and placed a compassionate hand on Ralph's arm.